THE SEAPLANE ON FINAL APPROACH

THE SEAPLANE ON

DOUBLEDAY NEW YORK

# FINAL APPROACH

*A Novel*

Rebecca Rukeyser

Copyright © 2022 by Rebecca Rukeyser

All rights reserved. Published in the United States by Doubleday, a division
of Penguin Random House LLC, New York, and distributed in Canada by
Penguin Random House Canada Limited, Toronto. Originally published in
paperback in Great Britain by Granta Books, London, in 2022.

www.doubleday.com

DOUBLEDAY and the portrayal of an anchor with a dolphin are
registered trademarks of Penguin Random House LLC.

*Book design by Anna B. Knighton*
*Jacket design and illustration by Jo Walker*
*Moon © Trevor Jones/Shutterstock*

Library of Congress Cataloging-in-Publication Data
Name: Rukeyser, Rebecca, 1985– author.
Title: The seaplane on final approach : a novel / Rebecca Rukeyser.
Description: First edition. | New York : Doubleday, [2022]
Identifiers: LCCN 2021026129 (print) | LCCN 2021026130 (ebook) |
    ISBN 9780385547604 (hardcover) | ISBN 9780593314029
    (trade paperback) | ISBN 9780385547635 (ebook)
Subjects: GSAFD: Humorous fiction. | LCGFT: Humorous fiction. | Novels.
Classification: LCC PS3618.U56267 S43 2022 (print) |
    LCC PS3618.U56267 (ebook) | DDC 813/.6—dc23
LC record available at https://lccn.loc.gov/2021026129
LC ebook record available at https://lccn.loc.gov/2021026130

MANUFACTURED IN THE UNITED STATES OF AMERICA
1 3 5 7 9 10 8 6 4 2

First American Edition

*For Florian*

THE SEAPLANE ON FINAL APPROACH

CHAPTER 1

The name Lavender Island Wilderness Lodge was honest, for the most part. The nearest neighbors were eight nautical miles away, the nearest Native village twenty nautical miles, the nearest town with a streetlight fifty. It was a lodge. It was on an island—one without roads, electricity, or any power other than that supplied by the generator. The staff wasn't allowed to use the satellite phone, except in the case of emergencies. But there was no lavender in Alaska; what grew best on the slopes of Lavender Island was fireweed.

I appreciated this lie. Lavender was a cultivated flower, in the way that gloves and small spoons were cultivated. Lavender Island sounded like a place that understood, even as it hunched in the middle of nowhere, that nature was a bear at the end of the garden.

The owner, Maureen Jenkins, had a practiced laugh and a practiced jauntiness: she insisted on being called "Maureen." Her hands, as she untied the mooring lines, coiled the rope, and steered the boat from the harbor, were clever. I believed that under her watchful eye I would be molded into a truly excellent baker.

Because that was going to be my job, Maureen explained. I was to be something of a domestic jack-of-all-trades, but she'd really hired me because of my enthusiasm when it came to baking. She told me that I would have a few definite tasks: cookies were essential for packed lunches, because people crave sugar at high latitudes. Pie was essential for dessert, because people needed to taste those fresh Alaskan berries. And bread! We needed fresh bread with fresh salmon.

She encouraged me to do fun things in my off-hours, like walk down the beach and hunt octopuses by luring them from their holes with syringes full of bleach. But life on a homestead was, Maureen reminded me, her eyes never leaving the flat water of the sea lane, more work than play. The guests needed continual attention.

·

It took the better part of four hours to navigate out from the town of Kodiak to Lavender Island. The journey was longer when the weather was inclement. But there was really no such thing as bad weather in Alaska, said Maureen, only bad clothing. However, it was true that days like today, with the water reflecting a high, starched sky, were the very best. Maureen turned from the wheel, pointing out a flotilla of sea otters, a whale breaching, a chartreuse green slope scattered with blooming lupine.

"It's a bluebird day, Mira," she said. "Perfect welcome weather for you."

Maureen, knee steadying the wheel, filled a thermos lid with coffee and handed it to me. When the Wilderness Lodge guests came in for breakfast, she explained, my job was to keep the coffeepot full, and to serve up the platters of pancakes and the bowls of eggs. In the evening, I'd fill the wineglasses and make sure dessert was plated even before the dinner was over. I would wear black-and-white-striped chef's pants. I would be quiet and bustling.

When I introduced the meals, Maureen said, I should tell the guests, "Tonight Chef has prepared for you . . . ," and then, whenever possible, throw in the word "Alaskan." It was impossible to overuse the adjective. The fish were Alaskan. The nettles in the salad grew native on Kodiak, Alaska's own Emerald Isle. We grew rhubarb in our Alaskan garden.

•

There were two girls jumping and waving on the beach of Lavender Island Wilderness Lodge. Maureen smiled as she anchored and tied up to a smaller aluminum skiff. The girls were the size of wedding cake toppers at this distance, with the same pleasant blurred faces.

"Polly and Erin," said Maureen. "I think you'll all hit it off—you all just graduated high school, and you all have the same sparkle." I hadn't graduated. I had flunked out, but I didn't correct Maureen.

Polly and Erin's voices rose up, reflecting cleanly across the water. "Welcome to Lavender Island," they sang, to the tune of "For He's a Jolly Good Fellow." "Welcome to Lavender Island, welcome to Lavender Island," and there they dissolved. They had practiced the first part of their welcome, but not the second. They couldn't say "And so say all of us," because there were only two of them. It was true that somewhere, in the gray clapboard buildings nestled in the alders, there were two more.

I helped Maureen unpack into the aluminum skiff and watched as she motored to shore. It was only a few hundred yards, but it was enough to hear the roar of the skiff recede and echo back to me from the mountain. As the motor on the skiff cut out, there was the sound of laughter. The word "Hi!" bobbled out to me.

In the brambles high above the Wilderness Lodge, I saw the haunches and triangular head of a bear. It was a surprisingly jolly sight: piggy snout, round ears, the movement of a seal in an aquarium. The only unsettling thing about the bear was its fur, which was the pale color of dog shit.

Then Polly and Maureen were back in the skiff, coming toward me. Polly smiled, waving both hands. "Mira! You're here!" she said, and I said, "I'm here!" When I looked back at the hillside, the bear was gone.

"I saw a bear," I told Maureen.

"The Kodiak Archipelago is famous for its bears," she said. "It's the real-deal wilderness out here, the kind of place that really molds you."

On the beach, Erin took me right into a tight hug. She was covered in auburn freckles and wore an oversized *Les Misérables* t-shirt. Polly was terribly pretty. Her cheeks seemed to be so full of cheek that they shone. She was small, with small feet. Erin's large feet were pointed outward, and she had a scarecrow grace.

I went to grab my duffel, but Erin wouldn't hear of it. I had just arrived, she could take it. She hoisted it and placed a box on top of it. There was glee in her movements; she was happy to exert.

Maureen smiled, and Polly and I took up the lead.

"She's like that," said Polly. "She's super-strong. And you packed light!"

"Did you know her before?" I asked.

"Oh yes," said Polly. "We've known each other since sixth grade."

•

Maureen's husband, Stu, shook my hand in mock formality, and then pulled me into a bear hug. As we walked up the path from the beach, he pointed out a driftwood sign shaped like an arrow and painted with the words "Beer Creek." It pointed into a small freshet. There were beer bottles nestled in the gravelly bed, and Stu picked one up.

"The bounty of Alaska!" Stu said. "Berries from the bushes! Fish from the ocean! Beer from the streams!" He punctuated this sentiment with a vigorous swallow, righting it with enough force so that beer foamed over the lip.

"I only speak English—and I can't even speak English that good," Stu said, "but I know 'cheers' in several languages."

•

On a calendar in the mudroom of the Big House was a list of all the guests coming to Lavender Island Wilderness Lodge— "Jaan & Co!" "Dennis and Ethel Anne!"—each with an exclamation mark. I didn't think that the guests would ever see the calendar in the mudroom, but they would have felt welcome if they did.

Passing through the mudroom, you entered the kitchen, where a man was busy frying onions in a thick layer of oil. He was skinny, and so tall that I had the impression his legs hinged at his waist around my line of sight. He waved, and then turned back to the stove.

Polly and Erin showed me to my bedroom. It had two beds and two windows that looked through a tangle of spruce trees to the flat expanse of the Shelikof Strait.

"Stu did his 'Beer Creek' routine with you," Erin told me.

"He always does that," explained Polly. "I was here last year, but you and Erin are newbies."

"Chef," said Erin, hopping up to sit on the chest of drawers. "Chef's new."

"The stuff he cooks is so greasy," said Polly. "He says people like soft food because it's easy on the teeth."

Chef's teeth were bad, they told me. The front ones, you could see by the blackened root, were no longer sturdy. While he was cooking, Chef spoke words of encouragement to his fish, his sausage gravy, his pans of rice and buttery greens. He enunciated so they could hear him, all his foodstuffs. "Yes," he'd say, or "Nice job," or "Brown!" to the onions when they browned nicely. When he tasted his meals, he used his molars to chew, inhaling in a way that sounded like he was taking a sip from a cup of hot coffee.

Polly and Erin and I sat in my empty bedroom until dinnertime. I could tell what kind of girl Polly was: extracurricular activities, round handwriting, spotless Adidas sneakers. I could see it in the way she massaged lotion into her cuticles. Erin, I concluded with some pleasure, was a big nerd.

·

We continued the celebration of my arrival after dinner, making s'mores at the fire pit. The Alaskan flag crackled from a pole on the gear shed. It was still light: a bluebird day at ten p.m. Chef arrived, sliding through the shale chips on the beach.

"Beer?" asked Stu.

"Stu," said Maureen.

"Oh, sorry, Chef," said Stu. "I forgot."

"None for me," said Chef, taking a seat on one of the driftwood benches. "Where are the marshmallows?" Maureen handed Chef a wicker basket.

This was to be another one of my chores, said Maureen. On all but the stormiest days, the guests usually ended up around the fire pit. After I'd finished doing up the dishes, I should pack up the basket full of s'mores supplies. The trick to my role was this: it was important that it looked like it was my idea. My role at the Wilderness Lodge was to act as if I was supplying goodies out of the generosity of my spirit and a desire to ply the guests, grandma-like, with sweets. Maureen encouraged me to say things like "I thought a salmonberry pie sounded like a good idea" when it was Tuesday. Tuesday's menu always called for salmonberry pie.

·

It had been decided that Chef and I would eat alone in the sunroom while the guests, Erin, Polly, Maureen, and Stu sat in the dining room. The reason given was that we had to eat quickly—to finish before the guests might want their plates taken away and their coffee and dessert served.

I could tell that the actual problem was that Chef was eerie, with his nicotine-stained mustache and his matchstick legs. He seemed to be partially deaf: he spoke loudly.

"I used to live in Pahrump, Nevada," said Chef. "A lot of hookers in Pahrump. Best paid hookers in the country."

It would be incorrect to describe Chef as sleazy; he was too enfeebled to be sleazy. Sleaze demanded fortitude, and Chef didn't seem to have any.

I watched Chef eat his s'more. To quell the emotion I had toward him—the kind of sad disgust you'd feel after seeing an ugly baby—I tried to imagine what I would do if I were him in order to have a better life. I would get new teeth, I thought. I would move somewhere warm. I would get involved with an activity that, although I might not like it, gave me hope and solace. The church? I could find a small, warm town with a good church. As I looked at Chef, I felt the great urge to confess myself, although I didn't know what it would be that I was confessing to. If I were Chef, I thought, I would probably want to die.

•

Later, I'd meet a lot of people like Chef: people who had looked for a better life teaching English overseas. A co-worker in my first EFL job—Business English at a Czech petrochemical plant—sat me down in the canteen and gave me some advice.

Half of all EFL teachers were adventurous, she said. The other half were broken. These were the losers: the floaters, the drunks, the people who got off on the petty power wielded at the head of a classroom, the people who couldn't get laid unless they fucked their students, and the people who found it impossible, for one reason or another, to return home.

•

I ended up spending most of my time on Lavender Island inside, in either the kitchen, the Bake Shop, or the Guest Cabins. I was the domestic. But my favorite chore was taking out the trash.

The food scraps needed to be thrown on the beach at low tide so everything could be washed away. And because the tide was always changing, I had to take it down to the end of the beach, where the comma of gravel petered out.

This chore afforded me a great dignity. The consultation of the tide booklet lent it a mathematical air. In the stretching twilight I was an adventurer, outfitted with waterproof boots. I was intrepid, braving the rain or the pink end or beginning of a bluebird day. In two directions, the mountains loomed up.

After I'd dumped the garbage, I'd sit and look back at the Wilderness Lodge on its spit, looking like the houses in a model railroad. The grass on the hillside was like the grainy dust model makers used to shadow the landscape of the railroad in greens and darker greens. Its smallness was comforting and had begun to take over my whole world.

As far as anyone on Lavender Island was concerned, I had only ever existed here, in my stripey pants. I was a nice girl from a nice home, with little in the way of skills and the past that shapes everyone—immersive games, immersive lust, a preoccupation with making our rooms our own, a hatred as vague as the thick end of a lighthouse beam that we swoop at anyone that crosses us. My ferocity was leveled at becoming.

## CHAPTER 2

A storm rolled up the Gulf of Alaska and turned the whole world blue. It was my fifth day on Lavender Island, the afternoon that the guests from Norway—Jaan & Co.—were expected to arrive by seaplane. But the Norwegians were stuck in the town of Kodiak, enjoying the comped accommodations at the Best Western. We were stuck inside. I had been given the task of cleaning the sunroom.

The sunroom was used for a few things. It was where Chef and

I ate our meals. It was where Stu and Maureen's dachshunds, Ruby and Judy, slept, and it was where the Lavender Island merchandise, mugs and t-shirts, was housed on a low counter. True to its name, the sunroom got very sunny on clear days: two full walls were glass, and there were two skylights. A large oblong window divided the sunroom from the living room in order to let some of the illumination pour into the living room during the darker months.

No one had bought a mug in a while, it seemed—there was a dead bee in one of them. Ruby and Judy snoozed in a pile. I couldn't hear anything over the rain pelting against the windows.

Through the window that looked into the living room, I watched Polly plump down in one of the big living room armchairs. Stu followed her in. He was talking, gesturing out to the storm with open hands.

At one point, when Stu spread all his fingers wide and raised his eyebrows in emphasis, Polly did a little flip in the easy chair and mashed her face into the armrest. It was clear that she was flinching at some gruesome storm story—I could almost hear the squeal—but when she raised her head she was grinning, eyes tightly closed. Stu, laughing, stretched out, and then took ahold of the toes of her white stocking foot and tickled it. Polly started shaking her head, and I could tell that she was saying, "Oh, no, no, no! No! Stop!"

Then I saw Stu step back, dropping Polly's foot. Polly, suddenly upright, feet on the floor. The rain against the windows was a different rolling rhythm than the rain against the skylight. A bright square appeared on the living room carpet; a light upstairs had been switched on. Stu walked to the staircase and spread his fingers wide again, this time in greeting. Erin walked down the staircase, gave his arm a friendly one-two punch, and he dodged her high kick. Polly lay on the sofa, hugging a pillow to her chest. I ducked down and straightened the t-shirt display.

·

The storm moved on and left a week of gray cloud cover. Jaan & Co. arrived, their seaplane humming low under the clouds. They unfolded from the seaplane with efficient grace, then helped push the plane back from the beach into the water before going to the Beer Creek. I was back in the kitchen, peeling potatoes, when they walked past. There were three of them, all tall, all with glossy beards, and they each took a separate cabin. There was something unimaginably wealthy about them and about the luster of their windbreakers, which appeared to be covered in some sort of fine wax or vellum.

Maureen knew the type. Norwegians were used to a rugged landscape: they had their own mountains and their own valleys filled with seawater. They were not to be impressed by things like staggering peaks and mentions of how cold the water was. What they wanted was America: the proximity of bears and guns. The Beer Creek was stocked with Coors Light.

When I had finished peeling the potatoes, I found Maureen and Chef bent over the week's meal plan: American at top volume. We didn't need to pick wild nettles for wild-nettle salad. We needed macaroni and cheese, billed on the menu as "mac n' cheese," topped with crumbled potato chips. In all likelihood, the salmon could just as well be canned.

Maureen saw me watching them and said, "Mira! Wouldn't you like to light some candles?"

Coziness was not in short supply on Lavender Island; little things were cozy because they came wrapped in such extremity.

There were always candles lit at mealtimes in the dining room, and candles lit in the evenings in the living room. We didn't need the light—civil twilight, the tide booklet informed me in a helpful key that broke the degrees the sun had slipped below the horizon into blue gradient squares, didn't start until after midnight. But we needed the flame. We needed the smell of burnt matches. We needed to be in the presence of the antique technology of heat and cooking and sustaining. We needed it like we needed butter in our oatmeal.

Maureen understood this, and encouraged it. She'd settle into her chair, curling her feet under her in the tidy way a cat tucks its paws under its chest. To see Maureen was to see the great competency of being a mammal. She nourished herself against the elements. The afghans in the Big House were made by her, evidence of maternal instincts, the frailty of the body, the long hours of darkness in which there was nothing to do but spend time creating something that would give an illusion of the warmth of summer.

"It's God's own country," Maureen would say. And that made me jealous, because I'd arrived at the same conclusion, except my conclusion was a series of wide-eyed thoughts that I'd never articulated coherently, only with words like "Wow" and "Oh."

Maureen said what I'd been feeling all along—a deep, solemn fear because the mountains were so steep you were aware of the fact that they were nothing but the tops of bigger mountains growing out of the sea, because bears were not only ferocious but real, because the water could kill you in fifteen minutes, not by dashing your head but by rocking you to hypothermic sleep, first cold and then warm. But I didn't have any way of explaining this immensity either to myself or to other people.

But Maureen could pluck at her afghan and look out at the land and say, "It's God's country." Her tone never faltered. But instead of being the high gloss of practiced dining room chatter and jokes about beers that grew in creeks, it was reverent. It was the same statement, again and again, with all the guests: the Norwegians and the fishermen from Florida and the young Vermont family, because she found it unwaveringly true.

By dinnertime, the fog had deepened with the fading light. I moved in and out of the dining room, bringing in beer and bringing in bread.

"What do y'all want to do most while you're in Alaska?" asked Maureen.

"In fact," said the Norwegians, "this is only our first stop of many. We go from Kodiak to Kenai, and drive up to Denali."

"The whole shebang!" said Maureen, and then, when they didn't understand, she said, "The whole tour."

During the course of the meal, Maureen became less folksy, primmer. She sat erect, talking about how she homeschooled her children right here on Lavender Island, and taught them to live righteously. Stu's role was to be hearty, wild, a stubborn man at the end of the world with an appetite for flesh. He was getting red-faced and slapping the table, telling his stories about Kodiak in the bad old days.

"Scraped his face right up on the way out—and that gangway was painted for traction. There was so much sand in that paint that he looked like he'd been in a losing fight with a cat."

The Norwegian sitting by Stu said, "Wow," and cracked another beer with evident relish.

"Twin boys," said Maureen. "I was thinking about building a schoolhouse, but the winters here can be so harsh that I was worried about bears going in and trying to keep warm. But it's truly God's own country, here."

The Norwegian near her also said, "Wow," and ate another slice of buttery potato.

"And here's some Alaskan venison," I said, bringing in the platter.

"Cheers, Chef!" said Stu, wiping his face with his napkin. "How do you say 'cheers' in Norwegian?"

"Skål."

"Skål, Chef!"

"Chef takes care of us so well," said Maureen.

"Chef's a real man of the West," said Stu. "An original cowboy. He's the real deal. Get in here, boss!" Chef came in and stood near the table, full of fear of being presented to the heft of these healthy Norwegians. They ate tremendous amounts without breaking a sweat—we'd have to prepare a lot of mac n' cheese.

"You'll have to tell us all tales of your wild past after dinner," said Stu to Chef, and Maureen said confidentially, to no one in particular, "He's a blessing."

Chef dipped his head in what seemed like part of a curtsy and then moved quickly back into the kitchen. I saw his dilemma: he knew that he wasn't supposed to talk to the guests, and yet he was being summoned. He stood rigidly by the stove, and then tucked a piece of potato into his cheek.

"I think I'm going to turn in," Chef said to me, and walked out the door. The screen clattered, and Stu roared from within the warm light of the dining room, "Chef's the strong, silent type."

I watched Chef's spidery silhouette get swallowed up in the dim patch of the alders.

I've often thought of Chef's fear of the Norwegians. Years later, I was hemmed in at a crowded bar in Beijing, making small talk with an EFL teacher who alternated between taking sips of his Tsingtao and clicking the rim of the bottle against his teeth in agitation. I was smiling, which is what I do when I'm agitated.

"I'm thinking," he said to me, "about what happens when you go north from Beijing."

"You get to Inner Mongolia."

"And then?" He clicked.

"You get to Mongolia-Mongolia?"

"But—and then?"

"Russia?"

He was looking up at the ceiling—he was so drunk he was looking up as if it were north. "And then you keep going," he said, "and apart from a few Siberian towns, there's nothing until you get to the North Pole. The fucking *North Pole*."

Maybe Chef had had some of this fear. The hale Norwegians came from farther north even than Lavender Island. Norway was farther north than anything imaginable. Thinking about the top of the globe was a bit like thinking about the size of outer space, or all the kinds of deep-sea fish still undiscovered, or the bears that lived on Lavender Island. It was doubly unnerving in the same way the bears were: one, because they lived somewhere inhospitable, and two, because they thrived there.

What I said to the drunk in Beijing was "It's God's own country up there." I said it slowly and solemnly, and he stopped clicking his Tsingtao against his teeth.

"A real Western dude," Stu was saying as I came in with more beer. "A real renegade. Chef's not one to talk about his exploits. He's a man of few words. But he's had a life and a half."

"Is he Alaskan?" asked a Norwegian.

"He is in spirit, that's for damn sure. He's as Alaskan as a red salmon in the mouth of a grizzly bear, but he hails from the Blue Ridge Mountains of Virginia."

"Chef is a good man," said Maureen.

Stu held forth. Polly was looking straight at him, smiling, her face as red and glossy in her admiration as Stu's was in the flush of his storytelling and drunkenness. Every gesture Stu made caused her eyes to flicker, and so he gestured more. Erin spent most of dinner looking at her plate, but she was listening, too.

"The Blue Ridge Mountains of Virginia—have you been there? No?—aren't blue, and they aren't mountains. We have mountains: you just have to look outside to know that these are *mountain*-mountains. But what they have in Virginia are hills. They're really pleasant, and there are farms and little creeks and places where you can buy things like fresh milk and local honey. It's charming.

"In fact, it's so charming that people forget about the dangers in these little blue hills. You can still get lost, you can still fall into ravines, and you can get attacked by panthers. And that's exactly what happened to five-year-old Chef and his mother.

"Here's something everyone in the Blue Ridge Mountains of Virginia knows: a panther's cry sounds like a woman's scream. And if you hear those screams, you start running. And as you run, you start stripping. You tear off your own clothes and you leave them on the trail, because panthers are either dumb or curious and will stop and tear apart your clothes, looking for flesh. Usually, you can outrun them by the time they've figured it out. Usually, but not always.

"Chef and his mother ran like hell, and, the way he tells it, they alternated between her stripping off a layer and her stripping a layer off of him. But maybe the panther had gotten wise to this trick, or maybe it was just too slow to run with a little kid—who knows.

"The panther attacked Chef's mom, and she, with her last bit of strength, pushed Chef and yelled at him to run. He did— he ran and ran.

"And here's the kicker," Stu paused, getting solemn through his shiny redness. "Before long, he came to a jacket, and then a shirt, and then an undershirt lying on the dirt road. And he realized something: that whoever these clothes belonged to must have heard his mother screaming for help. And whoever these clothes belonged to had followed the same advice as Chef and his mom, the same advice everyone in the Blue Ridge Mountains gets: if you hear a woman screaming, run, and take off your clothes as you run along."

"But there are no panthers here," said the Norwegian.

"No," said Stu. "There are bears. And there's no warning

scream when it comes to bears. They'll roar, but it'll be the last sound you hear."

Chef wasn't from Virginia. He was from Nevada; Stu knew this. But the Norwegians were invested in the dangers of Alaska, and to first hear a story about a ferocious big cat—the cousin to lions and tigers—and then to hear that the bears of Alaska were even more ferocious, mollified them. Panthers screamed; bears were the strong, silent type. Chef's swift exit, his stalking gait as he ran up to his tent cabin, were explained away. His haunted demeanor was nicely wrapped up in childhood trauma, and his childhood trauma was nicely wrapped up in the feral American landscape.

CHAPTER 3

I had been to the Kodiak Archipelago before. The previous year, I had been sent to spend the summer with my marvelous aunt.

My aunt, when she explained where she lived, would make her hand into a map of Alaska. You make a fist, and then stretch your index finger and thumb out. Your index finger becomes the Aleutian Chain (fingertip west, stretching into the Bering Sea), and your thumb becomes the Alaskan Panhandle (thumb tip south, pointing toward Vancouver). Where she lived was just below the second knuckle of the index finger, on the island of Kodiak.

I was sent to my aunt's cabin because it was thought that Alaska would correct me. My parents thought I was wayward, because my grades were poor and, even though I was a junior in high school, I still had no idea what I wanted to do with my life. I had no drive. But I hadn't really dabbled in delinquency. I had never gotten it quite right—I bought the wrong hoodie, etc.

So I was being sent away from the yellow California summer for being dissolute when I had only committed the crime of being interested in the dissolute: I was focused almost wholly on the subject of sleaze.

What was sleazy? I didn't quite know, but I studied everything for traces of it. Sleaze had something to do with sex, something to do with danger, but it also had something to do with other, more occluded, aspects of adulthood.

I couldn't define sleaze; I couldn't anticipate sleaze. But I could identify it. Places like dive bars exuded it, but it could also occur in sterile environments. Sometimes, even in Starbucks, there would be a man with a particular paunch that strained his shirt in a beguiling way, or a woman tottering in cork heels. Then, even the cranberries in the scones would twinkle with sleaze.

I knew sleaze had something to do with excess, and because of that I wanted very, very much of it. I approached the subject with a taxonomist's dedication. I made lists of sleazy things, and things that other people thought were sleazy but weren't, like:

*Cold weather, as opposed to hot weather, was sleazy, because the streets were empty and there was more privacy.*

*Cleavage was sleazy but breasts were not, themselves, necessarily sleazy.*

*Big rigs were sleazy, but so were four-door sedans.*

I made these lists when I should have been studying; I failed French. I was lost in a complicated maze of my own fashioning, almost seventeen, still biting my nails down to nubbins as I cataloged.

.   .   .

The word sleaze doesn't come up often when you're teaching English. I've only had students ask for its definition a few times, usually because someone on some forum has called someone else a sleazebag or said, "Take it sleazy." When asked directly, I've made the elaborate shrug that communicates that I am not a dictionary; the definition can be looked up.

But that's not exactly true. When I see students googling, finding pictures of wide lapels and five o'clock shadow, I have the sensation of a drawstring being yanked closed. That's not all sleaze is. But I can't fully explain about sleaze. I can't write on the whiteboard:

> *Fruit candy fed into female mouths and colored Christmas lights out of season are both sleazy.*
>
> *Sleaze can't exist without proximity to danger.*
>
> *People believe Florida is the sleaziest state, but they are wrong: it is Alaska.*

.   .   .

My marvelous aunt had lived in Alaska for ten years, which, she said, made her Alaskan, but she never failed to remind people that she was born in Apple Valley. She wanted to be authentic.

So the exchange would go like this:

"Where are you from?"

"I'm Alaskan now, because I've lived there for ten years, but I'm originally from California."

There was still something of the desert about my aunt. She knew it and tried valiantly to work against it. She set to enduring the cold of her first Alaskan winter by refusing to wear anything except a barn jacket until it hit twenty degrees. She had a patch of frostbite on one of her fingers that still bothered her, because she had also tried to go without gloves until it was twenty degrees. She hadn't thought about the wind chill, because she knew nothing of wind chill.

For her, this was a badge. Alaskans had bad hands: burns from fires, mangled thumbs from power tools, bent or amputated fingers from the hulls of skiffs clattering together in a sudden swell.

My aunt was so adamant about maintaining authenticity that she wouldn't dare categorize the patch on her finger that was only numb and a little mottled, like tripe, as even vaguely similar to the missing fingers caused by unloading aluminum skiffs in a storm. Hers was a rookie mistake; something that she liked to call "tax."

"Mira will pay the tax," she said to my parents, but she was talking about a gentler taxation than frostbite. Maybe skinned knees were my tax, or callused hands, or just the wholesome boredom that comes before learning how to make your own fun as surely as sweats come before a fever breaks. They sat at the kitchen table, discussing my future. My aunt lived in the town of Kodiak nine months out of the year but summered in the authentic wilderness down on Alitak Bay.

"You'll send her to spend the summer with me out at the cabin, and I promise: all the nature and the hard work and the midnight sun and the puffins, they'll give her drive. I promise I won't let her get too scraped up."

My aunt could have promised all the scrapes in the world and I would have thought her all the more marvelous. When my parents weren't listening, she promised she'd tell me about riding the rails.

"The story involves a poker game gone wrong," she whispered, and I would have exchanged my sensitive pinkie finger for her frostbitten one if only I could have heard the story then and there. She drank beer from a can, which I believe was also one way of staying authentic.

When she had been younger, my parents had considered my aunt tragic. For them, she'd held the same muted horror as the events on the local news: a missing child or a contamination in a nearby water source. She had spent her youth first on a casual commune in Arizona, and then trimming marijuana in Humboldt County.

But in her mid-thirties she had gone north to find a domestic life of her own. My parents nodded approvingly and repeated what they'd heard about the ratio of men to women in Alaska: the goods were odd, but the odds were good. They were pleased with my aunt's decision. But they fretted because they thought she had waited too long.

And in a sense—my parents' sense—she had. She fell in love with a man who already had a son and who didn't want more children. He was a safe, steady man and loved her deeply. She accepted his proposal. From what my parents told me, he was the first safe, steady man she had had in many years. By marrying him, she made it to comfortable middle age without falling through the cracks completely.

Both my parents and my aunt had rules about living your best life: my aunt called this authenticity, and my parents called it propriety.

These aligned on the subject of sending me north to Alaska. It was authentic to learn how to handle an axe and feed a potbellied stove, and it was an act of propriety to send a child who showed symptoms of waywardness off to Alaska. It was authentic to eat fish that you'd cut and gutted; it was an act of propriety to teach a teenage daughter—because my parents believed that teenagers had no real comprehension of mortality—that things died and you ate them.

"We're all grateful," said my parents, which was a cue for me to thank my aunt. I did, instantly and profusely, and then went back to the business of sliding my foot in its sock along the seam that ran across the linoleum kitchen floor.

I was nervous that Kodiak would be too outdoorsy to be sleazy, because sleaze, as I understood it, mainly occurred indoors, often in kitchens. But it was decided: I would go up in June. My aunt gave me a handshake when she left my parents' house, and told me to keep my nose clean and to buy long underwear.

·

It was early July when Ed arrived at the cabin. My aunt and I had already been there almost a month and had settled into a routine of painting the buildings, feeding the chickens, and taking rides in the skiff to visit neighboring summer camps and year-round homesteads.

That morning, my aunt and I were busy preparing for the arrival of both Ed and his father, my aunt's husband. I had been given the task of splitting kindling to feed the potbellied stove, and I heard the buzz of the propeller before I saw it. And then, with the same immediacy as all things that appear in the sky— it's not there and then it is—there was the miraculous shape of a yellow seaplane that dashed first right across the mountains, then swooped back left, then another right. It motored toward land, pontoons bobbing and propeller slowing. Then Ed, wool pants tucked neatly into Xtratuf boots, hopped into the water.

Ed was my step-cousin and, of course, looked nothing like

me or my aunt. We had merry cheeks and Ed had sharp cheekbones. We had full sets of teeth, and when I knew Ed—for the four days I knew Ed—he was missing one of his incisors. His gumline where the tooth was gone was the color of jam. He touched his gumline softly, prodding it with the tip of his tongue, sucking it with a little snap.

Ed had his duffel bag over one shoulder, and he slung his father's over the other. When he dropped them down onto the cabin porch, his sleeves lifted. His tattoo—an anchor—was mottled blue ink: there were blue veins straining the skin of his arms. Ed was twenty-four. He was a commercial fisherman; in the winter he'd go Bering Sea crabbing.

"Oh, Ed," said my aunt. "Your poor tooth. I hope you can still eat pancakes." She slung her arm around her husband's waist, and they went into the cabin.

Ed took a pouch of Top out of his pocket.

"Smoke?"

"I'll watch," I said.

Ed sat on a pale piece of driftwood. I stood in front of him. He squinted against the light, tapping the brim of his baseball cap. He propped his elbows on his spread knees as he rolled his cigarette.

"What happened to your tooth?" I asked.

Ed picked a thread of tobacco from his lip. "I was wasted. I called this guy's girlfriend a slut."

"Slut": a walnut word. The sound of a hatchet crack or a mouth sucking where a tooth should have been. Ed raised his eyes to mine, then over the top of my head, down my body, and back up to my head. I watched his eyes shift up and down; he took the cigarette from his mouth with his thumb and forefinger, swung one of his legs in toward the other and then out.

He was, I thought, sleazy.

Ed took us out on a skiff ride. I sat with my aunt while he stood at the stern, speeding and slowing and driving into the chop, making the bow crash down. Once, it crashed down too hard, and I clutched at the aluminum bench. Ed smiled, and turned around to hit the chop again at a higher speed.

Every evening, we all played poker around the kitchen table with whichever neighbors we called on the VHF radio to join us. Ed's father covered the plastic tabletop with picnic-print cloth, like the felt at a casino. I was slow to learn, and Ed made fun of me. Once I said that "twos" would be wild.

"Deuces wild," he had said, at the other end of the table, looking up at me. "You're going to break Vegas one day, little girl."

Everyone laughed; I laughed longer, with a hot face. Ed looked at me laughing; I laughed on.

I went salmonberry picking with my aunt, and we made a pie—she was teaching me how to make the perfect crust. It was our last night all together; Ed was flying back in time for cod season. By the time the pie had cooled, we were into our fifth round of poker, and it was the dark of nautical twilight.

I cut slices of pie for my aunt and uncle. Reflected in the window I could see half of the anchor moving under Ed's t-shirt. I asked Ed's reflection, "Ed, you want pie?"

"Yeah, that would be good."

I cut another piece and put it on a plate. I had my back to everyone, but I could hear the slippery sound of cards being shuffled. My uncle said something, and my aunt and Ed laughed, and the cards went slip, slip, slip. I ran the tap and drank a glass of water. In the kitchen window was the white whorl of the gas lamp, and underneath, the reflection of everyone concentrating on their cards.

I quietly stuck my middle and index fingers into my mouth and sucked them, drew them out wet. I peeled back the crust of the pie with the serving knife and stuck my fingers into the berries, then sucked them clean again. I patted the crust down with the knife and handed the plate to Ed.

He looked up at me, smiling with his lips closed. I folded the next hand early. In the black window, I watched him flick with his tongue where the space between his teeth was.

I lay in bed that night and watched it again, the fork in the last bite of pie, the shine of his fingers on the plate, the soft noises as his mouth worked over his missing tooth. I lay with a pillow between my legs and listened to the cabin settle, the breathing and bedsprings in other rooms, and the water lapping on the beach.

At breakfast, my aunt was worrying back and forth through the cabin. The coffee was boiling over. I was sitting across from Ed, occasionally staring at him, moving my eyes away before he could see I was looking at him.

"Do you want to bring anything back to town, Ed?" my aunt called from the other room.

Ed looked directly at me; I looked back. "Yes," he said.

I looked down at the table, my mouth open.

After that, he left in another brilliant yellow kiddie toy of a plane. Ed walked off the beach, and the plane skidded across the water and up. Once the sound of the plane was gone, I went back into my bedroom, masturbated, and then curled up in the army blanket and went to sleep.

·

After Ed left, I became oblivious in my lust. I wore baggy men's trousers, like my aunt, because they were sturdy and easy to bend and work in, and in those sunny days after Ed took off I would roll the waistband down so they hung underneath my hipbones and I would sprawl on the beach, kicking at the shale with my Xtratufs. I must have looked like a cat. But all I knew then was that the sun-warmed shale was too hot on my back, so I needed to wriggle, and that I was also wriggling as I looked up into the sky until the sun burned little wriggling fibers that floated down across my field of vision.

My hips swung at the memory of him as if held between two hands. I arched against any surface that would take it—when we were docking the skiff the lip of the hull hit steadily against my pelvis with the movement of the water. I crossed my legs very tightly, and I kept squeezing them.

I had never been a superstitious girl, but my mind cast around wildly, and I thought of attempting some sort of alchemy to get Ed back to the cabin. Were there any of his cigarette butts around? I would have put them in my mouth. That might achieve something—his sudden return. When I closed my eyes, I could see Ed's mouth sucking gently on the socket of his missing tooth.

I thought of all the things I knew about him. Ed didn't like eggs; he liked sweet things. This had shocked me at first, because I'd thought a hallmark of masculinity was the rabid desire for protein. But maybe, I thought, sleazy men stopped wanting protein and desired, instead, Dutch pancakes and pie. Maybe it was only limp, unsatisfied men who rolled up the sleeves of their business shirts and tucked into steaks at steak houses. Sleazy men who worked the cod season, the Bering Sea crab season, needed sugar. They were starved for the domestic, the sweetness of baked goods.

So I worked my way through the cookbook at my aunt's cabin. I folded a dishcloth into the waistband of my pants. I made sourdough from an ancient starter in a jar. I made whole-wheat bread and crumbles and more salmonberry pie. I learned a latticed crust. I learned egg washes.

I didn't eat much of what I baked. After all, men who were overfond of protein were soggy and effete; I had determined this truth. This suggested that women who loved sweet things were, by the same logic, loutish.

I started eating my eggs underdone, almost raw. I ate seconds of fried halibut. I spoke to my aunt and uncle about my desire for carnage. I ate the roe sacks from the salmon's bellies. I wanted, I announced, to go deer hunting.


My uncle was a quiet man who wore cable-knit sweaters and had eyes the same shade as his son's. That was the most interesting thing about him, to me: he suggested the rough outline of who Ed would become. Hair that grayed at the temples first, a face that looked okay if a little neutered with a beard, fingernails that hadn't become ridged and striped with age, thank god. What I felt for Ed was based on reckless fidelity. I had decided to move to Kodiak after graduation. I would be eighteen then, and I would become Ed's wife.

I often asked my uncle about his son. But because I was determined to be terribly casual about it, I asked him many other questions as well. I made a rule: for every fifteen questions I asked that were not about Ed, I could ask one question about Ed. I was told a lot about the town of Kodiak in the eighties, about the boom years of the fishing industry, about the flora and fauna of Kodiak. My uncle's voice got plummy when he talked about his bygone youth.

We sat out on the aluminum skiff in the fading afternoon light and fished for halibut—Why do you have to hit them on the head with a hammer?—and took walks up to the top of the mountain. We scrambled around the clusters of alders before getting above the tree line, where the mountainside was so steep that you had to crawl, using clumps of heather as handholds to pull yourself up. From the top of the mountain you could see the curvature of the earth. I spent most of my time following after him, counting how many questions I had asked him that weren't about Ed.

This is how I remember our conversations: me, depressed in an itchy way by all the talk of youth from someone who would never be young again, and then the mentions of Ed, which rang out like gunshots and made the world into something vast and sexy. A puffin flew low over the water, and my uncle mentioned Ed and then—bang—the puffin was now something connected to Ed. The heather at the top of the mountain was turning autumnal in late July, and my uncle mentioned Ed and—bang—the heather had something of Ed in it, something of bar fights that led to missing teeth, something of the muscular sound Ed made when he swallowed, something sleazy.

One evening, while I was making dinner, my uncle was talking methodically about whatever I had asked about while I was waiting to ask about Ed. He was sitting at the table, and I was standing against the cabinets—one of the cabinets had a round glass knob that fit almost perfectly into the dimples at the small of my back in the same way that a red-and-white restaurant mint fits almost perfectly into the dome of your hard palate.

I kept moving from side to side, the knob almost filling in

the hollow in the muscle and then sliding with a clunk over my spine to the other hollow. What made me aware of my own movements was the fact that my uncle was tracing the patterns of the plastic tablecloth to the same tempo I was moving. This was no surprise; after all, it was the same tempo as the little waves against the beach.

But, in the same moment I noticed my uncle's hands on the table, or maybe a minute afterward, my aunt was standing in the doorway. She saw me leaning with my back arched, sliding back and forth against the cabinet doors, while her husband sat at the table, hunched, his fingertips moving in time to my movements.

At dinner, I chattered on about nothing. The night was light, the buoy clanged out on the water, and I ate seconds of salmon because it would make me especially feminine in Ed's eyes.

The next morning, my marvelous aunt explained to me that her husband needed to return to town for the duration of the summer. I was not affected; I told him to say hello to Ed for me, and I told my marvelous aunt I would make more salmon for dinner. I had the entire day to myself.

. . .

I lay in the bed that Ed had slept in and thrashed around. I took what I believed was his pillow and licked it. I searched the drawers for something I could link to Ed and to sex, and came across a piece of foil that was probably from a candy bar but could potentially have come from a condom. I sat down on the edge of the bed with one hand furiously down the front of my baggy Carhartts and stared at the bit of foil in my other hand until I came.

I ran downstairs, afraid that my aunt had returned. But there was no sign of her. I straightened up Ed's room, stroking his pillow with affection, and took a shower.

Outside, the sky and the water were the same color as the tarps that covered the spare outboard motor. There were puffy clouds in the sky. The slopes of the sheer green mountain were fuzzy with lupine. I was all alone, and nature was benevolent, and I was beautiful. I was not only beautiful, but I was young. I was not only young, but I had found it, somehow: whatever I had lacked before, a focus that my well-meaning elders had called drive and seemed to me to be, simply, the inevitability of things.

There was time enough to accomplish anything I wanted, and pleasure enough to enjoy whatever happened before accomplishment. I looked at the clock: it was only eleven a.m. It was eleven on a midsummer day, and I was all alone. I grabbed Ed's blanket, walked to the beach, took off all my clothes, and lay down.

The shale was warm, and each scrabble of my bare feet as I lay there sounded like cocktail party chatter. I could see the sun from under my eyelids. I turned around and nuzzled against Ed's blanket. The smell of the wool and the seaweed combined to smell a little like sex. I slept so hard that I woke up with bits of wool tatting stuck to my face and the foil compressed in the inside of my palm. The sea was still lapping, and when I shifted, my feet still chattered the shale chips. The sun didn't appear to have moved.

By the time I heard my aunt's boat, I had set the table for dinner and the salmon was lying in an oiled dish, covered with lemon. She transferred from the larger vessel into one of the little aluminum skiffs, and I helped her tow it up the beach and secure it. My back was already tight and itchy.

She dropped her rucksack in the middle of the floor and I served up the salmon. She noticed, as we ate, that I pulled my sweatshirt back and forth against my back.

"What's wrong?" she said.

I said, "I laid out in the sun too long, and I think I got burned."

"Let me see," she said. "Let me take a look. There's aloe in the bathroom." I raised my shirt.

"You're crispy," she said.

My aunt balled her paper napkin and laid it on the tablecloth. She went to the bathroom and plugged the drain and turned on the water. I could smell the geranium oil in the bath.

"You'll want to soak, and then you'll want to scrub," she said as she came back to the table and took another bite of salmon.

"Aloe?" I said.

"Aloe later," she said. "No wonder you burnt to a crisp. You're so pale. You're like a china doll."

Here's the reason I give for what my aunt did: the lack of a white stripe crossing my red, bubbly back. What she had been thinking, on the way to town to drop off my uncle, on the way to the cabin, alone, was of my sluttishness. And here was my back showing sunburnt proof of naked sunbathing and that radiated heat like a crotch.

As I lay in the bath, watching the beads of geranium oil on the water and listened to the crackle of the conversations over the VHF radio, I felt perfectly happy. My aunt had lit candles and turned off the lights. The window of the bathroom looked up at the mountain, with its alders rustling in the wind.

There was a knock on the particleboard door, and my aunt asked if she could enter.

"I can scrub your back," she called. "You need someone else to do it."

I couldn't say no, because I was too polite to say no. Plus, there was that warmed brandy sound in my marvelous aunt's voice, that opulent comfort: she would scrub my back and help me heal.

She didn't look at me, shielding her eyes as she walked around the bathtub in an exaggerated manner so I could see how dedicated she was to preserving my modesty. She had hung the bath products up on a series of hooks above the bath—a caddy for shampoo, a sponge, and a brush on a long handle. It gave the bathroom the coziness of a ship's cabin or a storeroom. The towels were hung in a similar manner. My aunt reached between the towels to retrieve the brush, and then she sat on the edge of the tub and unscrewed the brush from its handle. Without looking at me, she twirled her finger in a gesture that meant for me to turn around.

"This might hurt, but it's the best thing for your back. I promise," she said, and she began to run the brush over the bubbled skin of my sunburn. I winced, and she said reassuringly, "I know, I know."

She ran the brush in the same figure-eight motion you'd use to stop hot milk from cooking onto the bottom of a pot. The blisters on my back dented and then broke under the brush—she started with light strokes and then applied more and more pressure—and when the collection of blister skin on the bristles started to affect the brushing, she dipped it in the water. I gripped my knees, and my aunt chanted, "I know, I know, I know." The tealights were winking in the water.

She changed the stroke from a figure-eight to the short, controlled movements of a paintbrush, running the bristles across my shoulders and then down in a stripe half a brush's width, pausing to extract the strips of skin from the bristles in the bathwater. "Ohhh," she said, "I know."

When she was done, she sluiced water over my back with her hands. Her shirtsleeves were wet with bathwater. I kept gripping my knees, and she got up without saying anything, pet my head, and walked out into the kitchen.

"Why don't you make a nest on the couch tonight," my aunt said when I came out of the bathroom. "I'll keep the fire going a bit. It's going to be cold tonight, and I want you to be cozy." She had brought me a mug of cocoa with marshmallows.

I believe—this belief comes in a whine, revving up like an outboard motor—that my aunt was a thief. I went up to Alaska that summer still retaining the essential understandings of childhood: (a) that teachers failed to exist in a real way outside of school, (b) that anyone who aged past twenty-five did so out of a lack of conviction, and (c) that my pain was the pain that stopped the world. My aunt took this away.

.   .   .

The next morning, I woke to the sound of my aunt bustling, lighting the gas on the stove and sliding the door of the particleboard cupboard open to get bread. I opened my eyes before moving or groaning and saw that there was a manic precision to her movements: she sliced the bread, laid down the knife exactly, put the slice on a plate, picked up the knife, and then sliced again. She saw my open eyes and strode over to me.

"How are you doing," she said. "How's the back?"

I had felt my back all night—the burst blisters kept brushing against the cotton of my t-shirt. But there was a bright perkiness to what she said that informed me that the question couldn't be answered with a complaint. Even as she was waiting for an answer, she rocked from slippered foot to slippered foot.

"Maybe some aloe now?" I asked.

"Aloe is the best thing for a sunburn," she said. "Aloe is the best thing for a sunburn."

She pattered off to the bedroom, and I heard the clatter of the cupboard being opened and bottles of this and that being moved. I took off my sweatshirt—it was an effort to stretch and get it over my head. When I went to lift up my t-shirt, I realized it was stuck to my back, and when it came off, it was spotted with yellowish stains.

"Here's the aloe," said my aunt brightly, and then, "Why were you sunbathing in the first place?"

"I thought it would be nice," I said, as she squeezed the aloe out of the tube.

"Nice," she said, and the whole panorama of my wantonness spread before me, stretched out shirtless on the beach.

.

For the rest of the time I was at the cabin, my aunt followed me, either with her eyes or with her feet. When I was in the garden, she sat in the disintegrating Adirondack chair in the corner and watched me weed. When I attended to the chickens, she was there with cupped hands waiting for the eggs. If I wanted to walk, I was allowed to walk down the length of the beach and no farther—she'd sit by the fire pit and watch as I went. When I made bread (or pie, or crumble, or scones), she sat at the table and talked to me. Or she'd be silent, smiling and shaking her head gently. I don't know who, in those moments, she was dismissing as a fool.

.  .  .

"Do you want to hear about when I rode the rails?" she said. My aunt rarely drank, but that night she was gulping gin. "Here goes: I started in Chico. The only other people in the boxcar were a nice couple of hippies a little older than me. We rode all the way into Illinois together: he had a banjo and she had a bag of weed, and we became best friends for the time being. He told me: you always have to carry a knife, and you always have to make a show of carrying a knife. Wear it in your belt, a big utility knife, and make sure that if you sleep you sleep on top of it, so no one can swipe it. The two best things to have if you're riding the rails are a big-ass knife, for the other train-hoppers, and a big-ass cross necklace, for the authorities. The same thing goes for hitchhiking: big-ass knife, big-ass cross."

I listened.

"You want to know the one time I got caught? It was in Elko, Nevada. We were all in a boxcar, four or five of us, and we had a party with a bottle of tequila and a Coleman lantern and were playing Oklahoma forehead.

"You don't know how to play Oklahoma forehead? You get one card, and you stick it to your forehead. You get to see everyone else's cards except your own, and you bet off of that. Well, the train ground to a halt, but we were still playing when the door slammed open and the flashlights caught us. The policeman arrested everyone but me—he said, 'High card wins, now get out of here.'" She took a drink of gin. "I bet he'd have let you off scot-free, too. I'm sure he would have."

I didn't say anything, so she snapped her fingers in front of my face and said, "Anybody home?"

I nodded.

"Oh, you think so, too. A little china doll like you always gets off scot-free."

I nodded.

"Nobody home. I guess I should let you get back to your book?" I had been reading *The Thousand Mile War: World War II in Alaska and the Aleutians.*

"Have you read it?" I said, to say something.

"No," she said. "I guess I'm not that fancy."

"Oh," I said.

"Oh," she said. "Well. I guess it's my husband's. He's the fancy one of the two of us. But you're not fancy. Here's a secret: you're a slut. You're a slut and you're getting fat. It's not just baby fat—you're not that much of a baby. It's fat-fat. Fat-fat-fat."

She came over and pinched my cheeks. "Fat-fat-fat." And she pinched the roll of my belly. "Fat-fat-fat."

The next day, my aunt slept until noon and then announced it was time to close up. I was supposed to go home in the fourth week of August, and it was only the end of the first, but there was no point in sticking around. She would stay behind and winterize the cabin.

A seaplane would come collect me early in the morning: there would be plenty of time to catch connecting Alaska Airlines flights from Kodiak throughout the day. She gave me fifty dollars in case I needed lunch or cab fare.

My seaplane arrived in the same motions—right across the mountains, turn left, double back right—as Ed's seaplane. The pilot, Sammy of Sammy's Air, was a cheery man with chubby cheeks puffing out from his beard. Also in the plane were two men who had just returned from a fishing trip—they'd come from a place called Lavender Island Wilderness Lodge.

•

I had parents that didn't believe in anger; there was no propriety in anger. But they believed in suspicion, and trained it on me. My aunt was, after all, cured. Alaska had cured her of her youthful squalor. My parents had never been wayward themselves, but they held fast to the idea that the rehabilitated were generous when it came to the faulty and tried to urge them onto the path of righteousness. My aunt, clearly, had found me too riddled with flaws to bother.

•

My marvelous aunt went back to her cabin in late September. Instead of taking the skiff—the weather had been so cold that the ocean had left a rind of ice along the tideline—she'd hired a seaplane. She was a competent woman who tucked her long underwear into the band of her soft wool pants and the cuffs of the pants into thick woolly socks, but that day, as she stood on the pontoon, as the plane motored toward shore, she was careless. She slipped and fell forward into the rotating propeller.

There was a possibility that the water had been too rough to safely land, but Sammy of Sammy's Air was a well-known bush pilot, and his safety record was impeccable. That line of questioning, along with the idea of a detailed investigation, was dropped. Sammy had seen it all from the pilot's seat. The windshield was spattered, as was the whole side of the yellow-painted seaplane.

What was Sammy supposed to do? He grabbed my aunt under her arms and dragged her from where she was lying in the shallow water back onto the pontoon. He radioed the Coast Guard: it was an emergency. He cut the engine. The Coast Guard choppers arrived within a half hour, but by then my marvelous aunt was dead, either of shock or of blood loss. The propeller had scored her from one shoulder down to her hip. Had she not died, she would have been paralyzed.

There was a quiet agreement that a woman like my aunt wouldn't have liked to live in that way. No one said it was for the best, but they believed that a violent death in sight of her own bobbing cabin (the sea really was about as rough as you could safely land on) was exactly what she would have wanted. She had lived in Alaska for more than ten years, which made her Alaskan.

·

My mother went to Kodiak for her sister's funeral; my father stayed to watch over me. I had gracelessly stopped participating in school. It was clear that I'd fail every single one of my classes, and my parents reasoned I needed supervision. Plus, a thousand-dollar plane ticket was a luxury, therefore a treat. Treats were to be withheld in cases of delinquency.

It's said that delinquency is easy. It wasn't for me. I had to approach it with a martyr's perseverance. But even during the most difficult moments, when the desire to do almost overwhelmed the desire to not do, I was spared from what I assume must be the most difficult component of being a total fuck-up: the feeling of "what will become of me?"

I knew what would become of me. I'd go back to Kodiak. I knew that things hadn't gone quite right, that a pulled thread somewhere had started a great unraveling, and after a bit of serious thought, I decided it had something to do with my incomplete and still-faulty understanding of sleaze.

If I could just do it over, I thought, if I could just have another summer, I could get it all right the second time around. Alaska contained more sleaze than the entire lower forty-eight combined.

So I'd written to a Mrs. Maureen Jenkins of Lavender Island Wilderness Lodge, inquiring after work the following summer.

Lavender Island Wilderness Lodge, a renovated original homestead, required a baker and a housekeeper. The tourist season lasted from June until November, Mrs. Jenkins told me, and they paid five thousand dollars, plus room and board. It was small, with only 160 acres.

That was fine with me; I felt in need of cloistering. I would spend all summer on Lavender Island, quietly figuring out everything there was to know about sleaze. Then, on November 1, I'd move to the town of Kodiak with my five thousand dollars and find Ed.

I wrote back to Mrs. Jenkins and boasted that my pies were excellent.

CHAPTER 4

The Virginians—Dennis and Ethel Anne!—arrived at Lavender Island three days after the Norwegians left. On their first morning, the weather was what Maureen and Stu called "soft." Looking out the window was like looking through a screen door: the gray air came down to the gray water, obscuring the mountains.

"There's a saying here in Alaska: there's no such thing as bad weather, only bad clothing," said Maureen, holding out a tureen of scrambled eggs to Ethel Anne. "We have a whole shed of rain gear—the kind that real-deal fishermen wear."

"Will we still see whales?" asked Ethel Anne. She was looking at her eggs, which were shiny with butter.

"The whales don't stop playing just because of a little rain," said Maureen. "After all, they have so much blubber. And your rain gear will be just the same: you'll be snug as a bug in a rug. Would you like more eggs?"

"They're very rich," said Ethel Anne.

"Oh," said Stu, "don't you know that calories don't count when you're on vacation? Our Chef, he's a real cowboy. He's from Montana. Eat like a cowboy; you'll have an active day and need a hearty breakfast."


Hanging on the back of the door in each of the Guest Cabins was a laminated placard listing safety measures to be taken against local dangers. I read it thoroughly. Lavender Island was a kind of seminary, I told myself: if I contemplated sleaze and its origins with sufficient rigor, I was all but guaranteed a bright Alaskan future. And I'd decided that something sleaze needed in order to flourish was a proximity to danger.

In the event of a fire, whether in the buildings of Lavender Island Wilderness Lodge or in the forest behind them, all persons were to go down to the beach. In the event of a volcanic eruption on the Katmai Peninsula, there was a trunk full of gas masks in the fish house, which were to be worn until the threat of ash inhalation had subsided. And in the event of an earthquake, everyone was to run immediately up the water supply line to the top of the mountain.

The Virginians weren't just tourists; they were aspirational. Together they were Jack and Mrs. Sprat. Ethel Anne was a plump woman who wore a string of black onyx beads to protect against harmful energy. Her husband, Dennis, had the face of a handsome Dust Bowl farmer. Back home, they had four little kids. Talking about them made Dennis beam, even as it drew the blood from his wife's face. They were equally animated, however, when they discussed the possibility of moving to Alaska.

"But the kids," Ethel Anne said. "A new start? A new school?"

"Our twins were homeschooled," said Maureen, and Stu glowed his grin in her general direction. "We wanted to keep them out here; it really is God's own country. But, from everything I've heard, the schools in Kodiak are tip-top."

"You'd be taking a risk moving to Kodiak, of course," said Stu, patting Dennis's back. "Preparedness is key. You get a gun. You learn to keep one ear open for tsunami warning sirens. Don't just stand there if an earthquake hits. Rule of thumb: if you have trouble standing, or it goes on for more than fifteen seconds, there's going to be a tsunami."

"Kodiak was completely destroyed in '64," said Maureen helpfully.

"You just *get*." Stu jerked his thumb at the sheer wall of green outside of one of the dining room windows. "You get to higher ground, and you keep going. Up the mountain, whatever mountain that might be. Just grab your kids and *get*."

"It's always good to wear a bell if you're going up the mountain," Maureen added.

"It's always a real good idea to wear a bell, especially after an earthquake. The earthquake can scare a bear enough that it comes out of hibernation. A bell alerts bears you're in the neighborhood."

"It scares them?"

Maureen and Stu laughed. "I wouldn't say it scares them, but they're not cruising around *looking* for trouble, the bears."

I listened intently to their conversation from my place near the sink. In the event of a true emergency on Lavender Island, I thought, we would probably just be swept out to sea.

·

The safety placards in the Guest Cabins had three illustrations, done in the pencil sketch style of a naturalist's notebook. There was a bear, peacefully poised to root through some berry bushes. The williwaw, a gale-force wind that came rolling down the mountain gathering speed, was depicted as a whorled cloud. There was also a pushki leaf with a manicured hand reaching toward it.

Pushki was a lesser Kodiak danger, listed below earthquake and fire and bears and hypothermia and volcano and jellyfish. It wasn't fatal, but would give you a brilliant, bubbly rash if you came into contact with its sap. Maureen showed me the first aid kit in the master bathroom and, next to it, a stockpile of calamine lotion and causticum.

My mood was buoyed by being around such a variety of dangers. *Find the danger; find the sleaze,* I thought, feeling like a hunter staking out a watering hole. But there was more: it wasn't just any danger that was important for the cultivation of sleaze. It was vital that the danger was considered with gravity, that the danger was respected, feared, and guarded against. My aunt, who had considered pushki rash a mild kind of Alaskan tax, hadn't kept any causticum on hand.

While Dennis and Ethel Anne settled themselves in Guest Cabin 2, I was tasked with cleaning the vacated cabins.

I vacuumed away fish scales and lint and beard hair, polished the wood siding with orange oil, and hid sachets of pinecone potpourri in the closets and under the beds. Maureen had taught me that the last square of toilet paper on the hanging roll was to be folded into a neat triangle; I folded it. Then I pocketed a Norwegian one-krone coin, a container of Tic Tacs, and a soft pack of Marlboros with three cigarettes left.

I opened the window to let in the smell of Lavender Island:

wet pushki, and salmonberries, and kelp at the tide line. I stared out at the dangerous water that separated Lavender Island from Tugidak Island and willed a fishing boat to come streaming by, hit a rock, founder, and need rescuing. Naturally, Ed was on board. His hair was plastered to his neck as I pulled him out of the water, and all his veins were as blue as his tattoo. Out here, hypothermia was a real threat, so we had no choice but to both strip naked and roll ourselves in a wool blanket.

·

There weren't a lot of decorations in the Big House. Hanging in the sunroom was a mobile made with driftwood and pieces of sea glass. In the afternoon, it shed chips of blue and green light on the dog bed and over the rocking chairs. There was a driftwood cross by the staircase. There was a chopping block in the shape of a dachshund where I stacked cheese cubes.

I don't know what kind of artwork was on display in the Small House, which sat at the top of the bluff overlooking the rest of the Wilderness Lodge. In the evenings, there was a light visible in the porthole that crowned it—Stu and Maureen slept there during the tourist season. In the winter, I was told, the Small House was kept boarded up.

The homestead was a small plot of land—you could reach any building from any other building within five minutes. But as I stayed there, the distances expanded generously. The Big House was quite a separate realm from the four Guest Cabins. The Bake Shop was different still. Chef's tent cabin was another place altogether: it was hidden away in the patch of alders behind the Bake Shop and the Greenhouse.

And there was the Small House, up on its treeless overlook. We weren't invited up there. It was Maureen and Stu's private space. I watched them walk up to the door of the Small House at the gray-lit end of the day. They seemed changed—Stu wasn't braying, Maureen wasn't laughing in the way that showed her back teeth. It seemed that only a great distance could make such a muting take place.

These days, when I'm overcome by feelings of distance, or when I just want to tour my memories, I take a drive on Google Street View. It's direct and immersive. Oh yes, you'll say, clicking on the arrow so your eyes jerk ahead. You remember this street!

There's the mini-mart where you bought candy with your allowance. Soon you're back there in full glide, a little achy, maybe, but serene. If you're me, you can stay like this for hours.

Then, if you're me, you'll emerge back into a service apartment in Ulsan, South Korea. The bright daytime streets are replaced by a kitchen lit primarily from the bulb over the hot plate and, from outside, the twinkling of the Lotte Department Store Ferris wheel. It's a good apartment: I can walk to my job at JSP English Academy.

Of course, there are places you can't access on Google Street View. You can't tour Beijing. Or the town of Kodiak, although someone's taken a nice 360-degree photo of the harbor. The street view car hasn't gone there yet. And of course you can't tour Lavender Island, because there's never been a car on Lavender Island.

.

It was three days until the summer solstice. We were all a little woozy from too much light. I wasn't sleeping well; I kept being launched up to the surface of wakefulness by thoughts of my brilliant Alaskan future.

Maureen had corralled the Virginians into what she called a "sunset kayak," even though civil twilight wouldn't start until nearly one a.m. Polly, Erin, and I were in the living room. From where I lay on the rug I could see Tugidak Island, its green slope ruffled against the grain by the wind.

"Fish poisoning isn't a thing," Erin was saying, holding out her hand for Polly to examine.

"Fish poisoning is a thing," said Polly. "There's a little red line, that starts from the cut"—here she touched Erin's finger—"and runs all the way through the veins to the heart. If it gets to your heart, you die. I'm not even joking."

"No."

"Yes. Did you cut yourself gutting?"

"Stu!" said Erin. "Is there anything called fish poisoning?"

"Absolutely," said Stu, walking into the living room. "No joke. Are you okay?"

"I have this scrape on my finger." Erin held out her hand.

"Let me see." Stu sat next to her. "Oh, you need to bandage that. Polly, can you get the first aid kit?" He held Erin's hand with one of his, and used the other to roll up the sleeve of her hoodie. "But it looks a-okay. If there were sepsis, there would be a line starting here, and going up the veins here and here, and eventually getting to your heart. But all your veins are blue." He traced one up her forearm, then traced it back down. Erin watched his hand, looking away when Polly appeared with the first aid kit.

"I guess Erin probably shouldn't take a hot tub, then," said Polly, stretching her back, arms out wide. "But I really, really need one. I'm so sore. Stu, can you turn on the hot tub for me?"

"Hot tub for guests only," said Stu. He was bent over Erin's hand, applying iodine with tender daubs of the cotton. "Costs an arm and a leg to heat that thing."

·

My work schedule was the same as Chef's. We were up at six. I made the pot of coffee and set the table. As everyone else woke up, we were busy prepping the breakfast and then the lunch for everyone to take on the boat, or on the fly-fishing expedition, or on the kayak.

Chef assigned homework: I was to read the sections about baking in various cookbooks. To make sure that I'd read them in full (and also maybe to make conversation), he would ask questions in the middle of our prep.

"What is the purpose of gluten?" he'd ask, and I would, without pausing as I grated carrots for the salad, say, "The purpose of gluten is elasticity."

Then, during dinner prep, when the sun hit through flower-patterned curtains, he'd either give me a little lecture—"Gluten develops when you mix the dough . . ."—or he'd compare the amount of supplies at Lavender Island to his last post, at a place called Mercury River Camp.

"Not enough malt vinegar, if we're going to get through to November," he'd say. "At Mercury River Camp, we had the big old five-liter jug."

What I decided about Chef was that he had failed in so many ways that the scope of his interests had dwindled down to what he could do competently. He was silent except when he could lead. When Stu played *Johnny Cash Greatest Hits* in the morning for the guests, Chef was elated.

"I saw him in concert," he told me again, beating cheese into a bowl of eggs. While the rest of us got tired of listening to Johnny Cash—the CD was one of five Stu kept in morning circulation, guaranteed to get the guests in the mood for rollicking—Chef bobbed contentedly along as he cut slices of butter and placed them between pancakes. He knew Johnny Cash; he was happy in his knowledge of Johnny Cash.

.

In the kitchen of the Big House I was Chef's subordinate, but the Bake Shop, a small outbuilding with a particleboard door located next to the Greenhouse, was my domain. I often marked a streak of flour on one cheek, because it made me feel industrious. It was makeup, though: a casual daubing so that anyone—Ed in particular, appearing suddenly at the door of the Bake Shop—would see me flushed, wanton, with a beauty mark of flour.

I liked to leave the Bake Shop in the eight to twelve minutes that the cookies were in the oven and go into the Greenhouse and touch the little sprigs of dill and the buds of oregano. Here was a pioneer's work, I thought. The movement between the Bake Shop and the Greenhouse proved how much there was to do out on the frontier. It could never just be one task at a time. From the Bake Shop to the Greenhouse to the laundry room, to tidying up the Guest Cabins, to taking the trash down to the edge of the beach. I was infused with a sense of being in train-ing; of preparing not just for the next task, and not just against the myriad Alaskan dangers, but also for my Alaskan future. It swelled before me, festive.

I would stare at the wall near the Bake Shop door and project moments from my life with Ed onto it, again and again, with a slice of tongue protruding from my open mouth.

I'd arrive on November 1: the hills are scrubby and brown; it's snowing, but I'm wearing a thin floral dress. We meet on the hillside overlooking the gray water. We meet at his house. We never make it to the bedroom. Instead, there's a lot of me pressed against the wall by the front door—his soft pants around his ankles, my skirt pulled up, my face mashed against the wall, one of his hands grabbing a fistful of my hair while the other uses my skirt as a rein—and occasionally bent over a kitchen counter.

What I knew about the rest of our future house was this: it has a picture window in the dining nook, made for staring down onto Kodiak Harbor longingly. He's a fisherman, after all, gone for long stretches of time on dangerous stormy seas, and I wait for his return with wind-whipped hair. I'm acutely aware of the dangers all fishermen face; my nails are bitten down.

Our house will be in town, I decided, because I was unsure whether sleaze could exist outside of a location with at least one streetlight. Sleaze needed to be observed; it couldn't observe itself. It's up to the viewer of sleaze to say, "That's sleazy." If you say, "I'm sleazy," no, no, you're not. You're a child in a raccoon cap playing Davy Crockett.

Projected on the wall by the Bake Shop door, I called my husband, Ed, sleazy in mocking tones, and he unbuckled his belt and told me I didn't know what sleaze was—not yet, I didn't. These were the happiest moments of my first weeks at Lavender Island.

.

Of course, even then there were times when I wanted, more than anything, someone to tell me it would all be okay. I thought about my aunt: a dream of her hand pinching at my belly fat, again and again and again, and then stopping with such force that I woke sitting upright. In order to get back to sleep, I would think about Ed and masturbate. I'd wrap myself in my blankets and find a glinting shard of sleaze and dream detail into it until it multiplied, expanding into the mosaic of my beautiful future, and I would embellish—what was the light like?—until they whirred with life that was so much more vivid than my own that I forgot to be lonely.

·

Was Richmond, Virginia, sleazy? Whatever it was, Ethel Anne and Dennis thought it was unwholesome in comparison with the homestead.

"How did you folks end up here?" This was an angular question, aimed low from Dennis after a day spent whale watching. Everyone was comfy in the living room; the dachshunds were curled on the carpet.

"We were kids," Maureen began, resting her cheek on her palm. "We were young and in love and in Wisconsin.

"We'd gone camping in the woods at Chequamegon for our honeymoon. We spent ten days up there, and when we went home, we were both a little blue to be back in the real world. I still remember when we decided: It was a hot August, and we'd slept in the living room with all the windows open. We woke up early—it was humid, and it was a cicada summer, terribly loud—and just lay there looking at the ceiling fan. We wanted to be cooler, to be someplace cold. We started planning a camping trip out in Montana or Washington State. It's all we'd talk about—Stu went to Triple A and brought back maps, first of the Pacific Northwest and then of all fifty states. We ended up with maps all over the dining room table.

"And then, one evening, we decided to get down to business planning the camping trip. Stu took pretty much all the maps in his arms, fifty Triple A road maps, and of course he spilled them everywhere. We had to crawl around picking them up, getting sweaty and dusty and angry. The last one—it had slid all the way under the sofa—was a map of Alaska. And we both stopped and looked at it. Just stared at the cover, because it had a picture of Mount Denali, and in front of it a lake with these spruce trees. It looked so cold and fresh.

"The next day, we went to the library. And within a week, we'd found out about getting a homestead. We were kids, of course—we just thought it would be like camping forever. But you know what: even when the weather got colder—even when it got really, really cold—we still wanted to make it. We were a couple of dumb kids."

Ethel Anne's and Dennis's faces were illuminated. There it

was: stupid youth. The same impulse that drove people to dance all night and marry without thinking of finances. It was as easy a thing to get up and move to Alaska as it was to fall in love: you just needed to be restless enough in your need, moved by something as small as a picture of cold, bristling pines.

"We got this place in 1975," said Maureen, and at that point she was just summarizing what it said on the website, under information about Alaskan halibut and Alaskan bear sightings:

> *We got this piece of land in 1975, provided by the U.S. government under the Homestead Act. We are one of the last American homesteaders, a tradition started in 1862. Homesteading is a lifestyle of self-sufficiency. In exchange for turning a patch of wilderness into our own piece of Heaven, we obtained the title of the land for free.*

"This piece of land was a gift from the U.S. government," said Maureen.

"Gift?" said Stu. "We worked our fingers to the bone for this place. Literally," and he held out his hand. "I lost the tippy-tops of both these fingers in a circular saw."

"We do have one or two war wounds," said Maureen, and

rolled up her sleeve and showed Dennis and Ethel Anne a scar running down her arm. "But I swear the paperwork was the biggest hassle. Every paragraph of that document starts with the phrase 'And be it further enacted.'" Stu joined in with her as she said this line.

Maureen turned to me; I was leaving the Big House to take the trash out. "You be careful out there," she said. "You might want to wear a bell for bears."

•

After I finished taking out the trash, I'd shower. I had my own bedroom, but I shared a bathroom with Polly and Erin. We kept it neat: our toiletries were lined up on a shelf above the bathtub. I used all of them, in a witchy turn, depending on who I would like to be like the next day.

Mine were pretentious. I'd picked shampoo that announced it smelled like freshness, and bodywash that announced it would smell like rain. I was going to be on the frontier, even in the shower. Erin had dandruff shampoo, which I thought was humiliating for her. Her soap was exciting: it smelled like grapefruit. In the middle of the steam, I read the copy written on the back. Mine promised alacrity, but Erin's promised nothing but cleanliness. It was boring that a grapefruit—a fairly sexy fruit, all things considered—would be reduced to its cleansing powers.

Polly had, predictably, I thought, a bodywash that was supposed to smell like a variety of tropical flowers, and shampoo that came in a bottle shaped like a little creature. It was a children's shampoo, and it smelled like strawberries. It promised nothing but fun, but I knew the spirit in which it was purchased. I had even attempted it myself before feeling like a fraud and giving up. It was like lollipops or gumballs or fruit snacks or stuffed animals. It wasn't for the boys, either. There was something about being a little girl for other girls, and being aggressive about it. These baby things that we persisted with, they were a way of saying, "I've been this way forever," or "This is what I'm known for." They were a claim to immutable personality. You couldn't, of course, come right out and announce it, though: that was as laughable as announcing your own sleaziness.

I used Polly's bath products more often, it's true. The sight of the shampoo bottle filled me with an achy rapaciousness: a little like shopping, a little like nostalgia.

Afterward, in order to mask the smell of the grapefruit or strawberries, I would pour out quantities of my own shampoo and bodywash. This served two purposes: it made the shower smell of freshness and pine, and if Erin or Polly ever said, "I'm running out of shampoo so fast," I could say, "Me, too." If accusation ever came my way, I would show my own diminishing supplies of fresh-scented shampoo and suggest that maybe Maureen was to blame.

I think no one liked Maureen much. I never paid attention to her unless she was giving us compliments. Then I paid attention, not because the compliments were pleasant, but because they had a certain glinting edge to them that you couldn't be sure of. It could have been an additional sparkle of truth and goodness, or it could have been cruelty.

She said, of me, "You have zest."

She said, of Polly, "You look like an indoor girl, but my goodness, you're a fisherwoman!"

She said, of Erin, "There's a way about you that's so bouncy, like Tigger."

To all of us, she said, "You're sparkly."

All these comments could be read as, "You're a slut."

•

Polly and Erin had decorated their shared bedroom. They had brought postcards and photographs, a few boxes of jewelry, a collection of nail polish, a stack of books on the art of fly-fishing and on Alaskan wildflowers. There was even a pashmina strung across one of the windows, attached to pushpins with loops of twine.

"Come on in!" said Polly. "We're just hanging out. It's really messy in here, though."

It wasn't messy. It was neat; the beds were made. The shoes were lined up. The only thing was that there was a line of Starburst wrappers on one of the bedsheets, and a crumpled large bag of Starbursts on the double dresser that separated the beds. I waited for a second in the doorway, sniffing a handful of my wet hair. I had used Polly's shampoo.

Polly didn't notice. "Are they talking about the Homestead Act again? That's one of Maureen's favorites."

"Stu talks about the Homestead Act too," said Erin.

"Yeah, but it's really Maureen's thing," said Polly. "Stu's into other stuff more."

"Like what other stuff?" asked Erin.

"Erin, why are you so interested in Stu?" Polly said. She smiled up at me. "Mira. Sit down. Have some candy."

Polly, I learned, loved biology. She knew how to fly-fish; she knew that it was an art. She knew about plants. She liked looking at them for long periods of time. She had been at Lavender Island the summer before and loved it so much she came back for a second year and brought Erin.

Erin had wanted to come to Alaska, she said, as a complete change of pace. Back home, she sang in the show choir and worked part time as an usher at the Arizona Broadway Theatre, along with her boyfriend. They'd planned to move to New York. But then they'd broken up.

And me? Why was I on Lavender Island? The sun came through the pashmina and Polly applied body lotion that smelled like sun-ripened raspberry. Erin was sitting on the floor in a lotus pose. I had the suspicion that they weren't too interested in talking about sleaze.

So I said, "My aunt lived on Kodiak. She was marvelous."

## CHAPTER 5

Polly knocked on my bedroom door, waking me up from a nap.

"Have you seen Erin?" she asked.

"She's up with Stu, checking the water line for leaks," I said.

"*Erin?*" asked Polly. "Erin is? Not Maureen?"

"I think Maureen had to do some paperwork?"

"That's weird," Polly said. "Stu had told me Maureen was going to help out. I don't think Erin's up to that, really." She started to flake some of the paint off the doorjamb with her thumbnail. "That's weird," she said again.

I'd come to the conclusion that there were three real states apart from California. One was Alaska. Two was Hawaii, because if Alaska existed then so did Hawaii. The third was Florida, out of sheer force of personality.

So it was a great stroke of luck for me that, after getting guests from dubious locations like Virginia and Norway, on the longest day of the year Lavender Island Wilderness Lodge was inundated with couples from Florida.

They came in, like a parade, from two separate seaplanes. There were four men, four jolly women. They splashed to shore in their waders, and one of the women sat right down on the beach and said that that was it, it was too cold, all she wanted to do was get back on the plane right now, right *now*.

"Just joking!" she said as a man who might have been her husband hauled her to her feet.

The Floridians stormed the Beer Creek. They wanted to immerse themselves in the cold of it all. The men kept pressing cold beer bottles to the women's necks, or lifting up their shirts and pressing them to their backs. Everyone squealed: the women because of the cold, and the men in affectionate mocking. They all kept dipping their hands into the Beer Creek and the ocean water itself and saying, "Brr! So cold!"

I was a little upset that they didn't wear floral-print shirts, because that's what I thought Florida was all about. But no: they were a flurry of flannel, and they all seemed horny. I had been called down to assist with their luggage—shiny Samsonite to a fault—and I walked behind a man who was walking behind a woman who may or may not have been his wife and I heard him give a theatrical "Umph!" watching her ass step up the trail to the Guest Cabins. She turned and flicked him with the water from a wet hand she had dipped into the Beer Creek.

The other thing they wanted to do was steam in the banya. Stu stoked the fire, and when the whole Wilderness Lodge smelled of sweet ash and boiling sap, he called to the Floridians soaking in the hot tub. "Banya's up," he said, raising his arms in victory. Two sets of couples rose from the steam of the hot tub with plastered hair and beery expressions. The women wrapped their towels like capes around their shoulders and ran, tippy-toed, into the banya. The men followed at a relaxed pace, ruffling their chest hair and steaming from their shoulders. The

door of the banya closed, and the hot-tub conversation continued, muted and amiable and broken only when one of the other
Floridians moved to the side of the hot tub with a splash to open
another beer. The blue light deepened half a shade; Stu piped
some Johnny Cash out of the loudspeakers.

Ten minutes later, the banya door clattered open, and the first
set of Floridians, ham pink and glossy, poured out, drinking
big gulps of the evening air. Stu materialized and said, "What's
really good—next time, what's really good—is going in there
with your shoes on, staying in a couple, three minutes longer,
and then sprinting down to the beach for a dip. It's good for the
heart," and he thumped his chest.

*No,* the women asserted, they couldn't possibly, they were
already lobsters, they were almost fainting in there. How could
they? And then the shock of the cold, cold water? But the next
group of Floridians was looking randy and conspiratorial,
already out of the hot-tub water with their flip-flops on, and one
of the women was bouncing up and down on her heels, and her
companions watched her breasts lifting and falling in her floral bathing suit. Fifteen minutes later, they were bursting out of
the doors of the banya and running as fast as they could in their
flip-flops down to the working beach. They scrabbled down the

shale, and then their yelps lifted up over the Fish House and the alders and down to the first group of Floridians, who were making their way back to the banya.

.

The extended daylight made the Floridians ebullient. It acted on them like amphetamine. They were mystified by the combination of sunshine and cold. They squirmed. In the evenings, trying to relax, they'd throw themselves back against the Adirondack chairs. The women would sit up quickly, fold their legs underneath them, and look surprised by their own sudden, flexible energy. The men gestured wildly with their hands. Everyone took frequent, deep gulps of air and had a postcoital flush. Their talks had an air of addled planning.

"There's no reason—no reason at all—why we couldn't set up something like this back home," one said.

"No reason at all!"

"People from up north would come down all the time."

"We could get a plot of land in the Keys."

"The *Keys*. That's exactly what I was thinking."

"No, no, no," said one woman, shifting to recross her legs.

"The Keys are absolutely saturated. What we need is something that hasn't been done."

"Absolutely saturated," they all agreed.

"But the Keys are beautiful," the woman added.

"So beautiful," they agreed.

.

I kept meticulous notes on sleaze. I jotted down things like *Glass bricks are sleazy but normal bricks are not* and *Sleazy: Formica kitchen tables, soft packs of cigarettes, thin floral dresses.* After watching the Floridians, I'd decided what made Alaskan sleaze different from the sleaze found in the continental United States. It was a question of light.

In the lower forty-eight, sleaze was compressed by the bookends of sundown and sunup. Nighttime was the right time. That's because sleaze fed on stricture. It was necessary for sleaze to be completed by the cuckoo—it was the *threat* of the cuckoo that spurred sleazy action on.

But in Alaska, daylight hours were more complicated. In the

summer, nighttime things—secret things, sleazy things—would necessarily take place during the daylight. The summer before, I'd assumed that gave permission for sleaze to carry on around the clock. What an idiot tourist I'd been. It was the opposite: in the height of a far northern summer, you needed to impose more order, fashion a fallow period for the sleaze.

*Or maybe,* I wrote in my notebooks, *Alaskan sleaze only happens in months where there's astronomical nighttime?*

The calendar in my tide book showed that, as of November 1, there would only be eight hours and fifty-seven minutes of daylight in the town of Kodiak.

On the second morning of the Floridians' stay, Maureen suggested that all three of us—me, Polly, and Erin—go help out on the halibut fishing expedition. I was mainly there to manage drinks and snacks and lunch: there were so many mouths to feed. We packed five thermoses of coffee.

Polly, experienced, was amiable and able, methodically spearing chunks of pink salmon on the edge of long-lining hooks and only occasionally clutching the railing for balance. But Erin made Polly look plodding.

I had observed Polly and Erin, both indoors and out. Indoors, Polly, compact, had grace. Erin was ungainly, with long arms that tapered into long hands. She was clumsy in her length—she made quick movements, and a limb, like a long, cracking tail, would knock over a Mason jar of pencils with a clatter.

But it became clear that Erin just hadn't been given the right tasks. She was too strong and too fast. Given an axe, Polly would chop and chop again, dutifully following the steps of the process like she was folding a cootie catcher or making paper snow-flakes. Given an axe, Erin would dash it through a log. It was beautiful to watch Erin chop wood. Her limbs clearly needed to be weighed down, given tasks deserving of them.

In the slow, nauseating swells that made Polly fish ginger candies out of her hoodie pocket and suck sulkily on them, Erin was alert and relaxed. Her arms were everywhere at once, and skillful. When a Floridian slipped hauling up a halibut, Erin caught him. With one long arm she steadied him, and with the other arm she grabbed the line.

Stu stepped next to her and took hold of the other side of the Floridian, whose boots were squeaking against the deck. He released the Floridian off to one side, and then, looping an arm around Erin's waist, helped her bring up the halibut. When the fish flipped over the rail, Erin took a step aside, as neat as a box step. She was laughing. Her face, framed by her drawn hoodie like a wimple, was full of the joy of relief—here, finally, was something strenuous enough for her to feel physically able. Stu stood aside and looked at her.

Then he snapped open the lid of a metal box and took out a large hammer. He looked at Erin again. He smiled, waving the hammer. "Ta-da!" he said. He squatted down and delivered a couple of stern blows to the halibut's head, stopping when a thin pink trickle of blood escaped from its gills.

·

The next day, Polly found me in the Bake Shop. When I was done making cookies, she said, I should come hang out. She wanted to talk about Erin.

Above Erin's bed was a collage of photos. There were maybe fifty of them, cut cleverly and fitted together in a jigsaw manner, decorated with scraps of foil and ticket stubs and a few candy wrappers. It had not always been like that, Polly told me. Erin had had a high school boyfriend that everyone knew was clos-eted. The two of them would sit on the lawn in front of the school and kiss and kiss without really grabbing hold of each other. The collage, which had hung above Erin's bed in her childhood bedroom, had been an orderly grid of printed photos until Erin's boyfriend had come out and Erin had been forced to cut him out of all the photos and add ticket stubs and foil stars to fill in the gaps.

He was, Polly confided in me, a member of the jazz choir. The fact that he was gay, said Polly, wasn't much of a surprise to anyone but Erin. When it happened—unfortunately close to the winter formal—Erin had mourned for a full month, and appeared at school after Christmas Break with henna-dyed hair and an air of aggrieved martyrdom.

.

My first impression of Polly was of someone beyond reproach or the reproach of sadness. She had a body constructed against sorrow. Big breasts, reined in with fleece vests. Small nose, black curls. A body that was maintained effortlessly with a sincere love of sport and the outdoors. I ogled her.

There is an exclamation that I'd heard from men who love

boobs: "Her tits are as big as her head!" It's a simple expression of comparison: three round objects, all a similar size. It's a little childlike—it's kind of like "I love you *this* much!" (arms thrown wide). This underscored what I believed about men who were especially drawn to big breasts: that they were simple and stopped at the first beautiful thing about a woman's body, perfectly happy to call it quits. The sleazy ones, I believed, went on from there and eventually found something more specific to be fanatics about. My own breasts were small.

"I shouldn't tell you, but she lost her v-card to him," said Polly. "Don't tell anyone, but she was hurt."

Who would I tell? Polly and I were seated on her bed, flipping through a stack of out-of-date magazines.

"I shouldn't say this, but I found her crying in the woods outside school. That's when I invited her to come here." Polly unwrapped a Starburst. "I knew she needed a change."

Erin didn't seem hurt; she didn't have any of the glinting pretensions of happiness that I'd seen in depressed girls. She didn't talk about how good her life was; she didn't proclaim epiphanies about identity. ("What I am," one tragic girl in my gym class had said before running laps, "is chocolate chip cookies and the blues.")

Polly explained that she had been close friends with Erin when they were children, but adolescence had provided a stark distance.

Erin was theatrical, a buoyant girl who would fold her body into curtsies when no curtsies were necessary (curtsies were never necessary). Polly's curls were never frizzy, and her pencil case was orderly; she checked over her homework for mistakes before handing it in. Erin, on the other hand, sang show tunes and did handstands.

Being around Erin had made Polly feel powerful and generous: she could have reduced Erin with one comment about her socks (purple) or her pants (too short), but instead she let Erin swoop her into a hug and told her to dry her eyes, her new red hair was cute.

"Here's what you should know about Erin," said Polly. "She's still really, really messed up by the breakup. In fact, I think she might be unstable, or maybe suicidal. I'm concerned. I think I might tell Stu and Maureen that she should go home. I mean, there are all sorts of things that could go wrong out here. The water can kill you in fifteen minutes."

.

What the Floridians seemed to want, besides exposure to the cold, was reassurance. They were sick of their state being the butt of every joke, or else the target of some tourists' fantasy of the good life. They were happy for someone else to take on that role. They wanted to commiserate; they needed to be somewhere that was also widely known as being less of a location than a collection of postcard views and fun facts.

"Alaska: where the odds are good and the goods are odd," said Maureen, and Stu said, "Oh, thanks, honey."

The Floridian women sat on one side of the table. The men sat on the other. Stu helmed the head, Maureen sat at the foot, keeping an eye on each other and the volley of conversation. There were enough people that Polly and Erin were set up at a card table in the sunroom, while Chef and I ferried trays of food.

"And here we have Alaskan venison."

"Well, you know what they say about Florida? Why couldn't

the baby Jesus have been born in Florida? Because they couldn't find three wise men or a virgin!"

Stu augmented his laughing by pummeling a riff on the tabletop. Maureen, setting aside her devoutness, crinkled her eyes and pantomimed laughter behind her napkin.

"Three wise men or a virgin!"

"And here we have wilted nettle salad with bacon dressing." On my way back to the kitchen, Maureen mouthed, "More beer."

The pathway curled around the Big House in such a way that, as I made my way down to the Beer Creek, I could see two scenes—one through the dining room window, and one through the window in the sunroom. There were the riotous Floridians, capped by Stu's mirthful bobbing head and Maureen, still hiding her disapproval behind the mask of the napkin. And, to the right: Polly's head bent over her plate, and Erin looking up at the wall that divided her from the dining room. Stu's laughter was probably vibrating the glassware.

•

"We have our fair share of characters," Stu said. "I could tell you a few stories from Kodiak back in the day."

"He could!" said Maureen.

"There was this guy, Jeremiah—"

"Jebediah," said Maureen.

"Jebediah. Jeremiah was a bullfrog, but Jebediah—" It was too late—the Floridians had started singing "Joy to the World." I had filled the Beer Creek and brought up another two twelve-packs and handed out the bottles. Maureen, her chin propped on her hands so her head was facing Stu but she could see me, mentally tallied the beer consumption.

When the Floridians calmed down, Stu gave a hearty "Encore!" but everyone was murmuring into their fresh beers.

"Jebediah the Mouse," he said. "Everyone called him Jebediah the Mouse. He wasn't quiet as a mouse, and he wasn't tiny like a mouse. He probably was pushing three hundred, all Irish-American bulk. But he had this really high, squeaky voice.

"He was a typical Alaskan story. He might also be a typical Florida story, too—I don't know from Florida stories. When I knew him, he was pretty much the town drunk, always perched on a bar stool at J.J.'s or The Cove, always looking ridiculous because the bar stools are tiny and he was a great big man.

"I grab a beer at J.J.'s, and Jebediah turns to me and says in this silly little voice, *Hey, buddy, you got any extra cash? I want a last one.* And even though the bartender's shaking his head like "No, no, no," I don't know, something about the guy made me buy him a beer and sit next to him.

"Anyway: classic Alaska here. The guy is some Ivy League grad—maybe MIT or something. And he decides early on to pull a Jack London and come to Alaska and find his fame and fortune. But he's a city boy: he has no idea what he's doing; he's taken to drinking with the deckhands and going to bonfire parties on Monashka Bay and not doing much else.

"Then, one night, after one of these Monashka Bay parties—young kids with too much disposable income, drinking top-shelf liquor on the beach and then passing out around the fire—he wakes up. He goes to take a pee, walking off from the other kids around the fire, out into the little spruce grove that lines the beach. He hears a rustle and thinks nothing of it, except that maybe one of the cute Kodiak girls has come over and he doesn't want her to see his Johnson. So he makes his way a little further into the spruces, where there's a clearing made by a tidal plain, covered in mist, the way it is in the early autumn.

"He hears a rustling again, so he turns back toward the spruces. There's nothing there, so he turns around again to unzip. There, lolloping over this silvery marshland, is this black shape.

"*It looked like a gorilla,* said Jebediah all squeaky, *but its legs were wrong.* And then Jebediah turns his hands around on the bar, like so, like jointed with the knees backward like a bird. Jebediah goes, *It smelled like death.*"

"What was it?" asked one of the Florida women, and one of the Florida men said, "A story to get free drinks," and the Florida woman held up her hand to silence him.

"Nobody knows. Jebediah says he ran back to the bonfire as quick as he could, and then he saw all those kids still asleep and ran to his car and gunned it all the way back to Kodiak."

"I would have gone back home," said the Florida woman.

"He was going to," said Stu. "But then he's telling this story one night at J.J.'s, and this old guy in the corner comes up to him and says, 'You know, that sounds exactly like this thing that was sighted up in Thomas Bay.' The guy that'd seen it figured he'd seen a demon.

"So Jebediah sticks around Kodiak, trying to find more information about these Thomas Bay demons, but there's not much. He starts drinking to get to sleep at night, he can't hold down a job, he's sleeping in his car as often as not. But he doesn't feel like he can leave. So I say, 'Why not? I would have run right back to Massachusetts or wherever.' And Jebediah says, all squeaky, *I felt like it picked me.*"

Stu set down his beer bottle solemnly, waiting. It started—the lighthouse of St. Augustine, the hotels of Palm Beach, a grave-yard in the Keys, all the haunted locations in Florida. Not punch lines, but snarled paranormal romances. That's what a popula-tion of runaways and peripheral sorts could provide: the ghosts beneath the palmetto plants. Another, more respectable, state could not boast of such riches.

I was seated in the living room while Stu held forth and the ghost stories began. There was nothing sleazy about ghosts, I thought. I watched the hands on the driftwood clock tick for-ward fifteen minutes: when fifteen minutes had passed, I should check who had finished their beers, ask who would like pie. S'mores were unlikely: the williwaw was blowing the alders silver side up. In the sunroom, Erin was holding her napkin on her lap and listening.

·

There are many men who have reminded me of Stu. It's a masculine asset to be the host, the mayor. That confident bonhomie is a kind of shorthand; it's short for having a big dick.

Later, when I was teaching near Prague, I met a woman who liked to discuss Rasputin; she harbored a barely concealed lust for Rasputin and only dated men who had big wild eyes. She said, about Rasputin, "He had a great big dick." No, I thought, but in all likelihood he was an excellent host.

•

During one of the late evenings of the week of the Floridians, Polly, Erin, and I stole and drank a bottle of wine. It was dessert wine—no one would miss it.

We drank the bottle of wine silently, passing it between us like pirates. There was an unspoken competition: first one glug, one round, then two, then three, and finally four, with our throats bobbing up and down with the effort of drinking that much Marsala. After we had rolled the bottle in an old shirt and stuffed it under Polly's bed, we leaned into what drunkenness we felt, enjoying the afternoon quality of the light even though it was past ten. Erin was lolled on her bed like a skydiver. Polly was cross-legged. I was hunched against the door.

Polly introduced it: "We should play Never Have I Ever." She splayed her fingers: jazz hands.

"Never have I ever done heroin," she said. We laughed with the mirth of the guilty. All our fingers were up; we had never done heroin, but we were naughtily drunk on dessert wine.

"Never have I ever been to Colorado," I said, and Erin thrashed in her bed. "Too boring!" she said. "Too boring!"

"Never have I ever had a threesome." None of us had ever had a threesome, and we held out two palms each.

"Never have I ever," said Erin, "smoked a cigarette." Polly and I each ducked a pinkie.

"Never have I ever," said Polly, "kissed a girl." Now Erin folded her thumb in her hand.

"Her name was Crystal," said Erin. "We kissed while listening to Loveline. She had Christmas lights in her bedroom." We both understood completely.

The scene made me nostalgic for a girlhood I'd never had. Three best friends, drinking sweet wine. The prism hanging from the fishing line in the window, and the jewelry hanging from nails, and the nail polish on the dresser, and the uneaten bags of fruit candy. We were sharing secrets in the fading light, laughing like sleigh bells, wearing colorful socks. I felt like I was getting an education.

These were good girls with proud families and without a desire to learn everything there was to learn about sleaze. They had played sports and had sung in the show choir. They had cut photos out of magazines and pasted them in notebooks for their friends and made photo collages on their bedroom walls. I had never done those things. But now, I thought, I could live all that girlhood within the span of one evening. The air was the color of sherbet.

"Never have I ever," I said, "drunk dessert wine." But, "Oh," I said, realizing it and leaning my head back against the door and laughing in bright bubbles, gripping the bones of my ankles, "But I have! We all have! Right now!"

"We have," said Erin. Polly laughed so hard she had to stuff her lacy pillow in her mouth. The water outside the window sparkled like nail polish, and the room smelled like the artificial citrus from the bag of candy warming on the windowsill. Everything was asexual but illicit.

"Never have I ever," said Erin, "given road head."

I had given road head. I folded a finger. Polly, blushing, folded a finger.

Erin gurgled her musical theater laugh. All her t-shirts were too big. Her purple socks had gold. Some of my comforting sense of superiority came back: Erin, I'd decided, was the least sexual person I had ever seen; her idea of sexuality seemed restricted to things like the idea of dancing the tango. Her ostentatious bodywash—grapefruit, the smell of new sweat—brayed loudly about the sensual. She didn't know, like I did, that sex was something furtive and shuffling and sleazy. That's what made it hot.

"What was it like?" asked Erin.

"Quick," said Polly. I was very impressed by this.

"What was it like?" asked Erin to me.

I had given road head to my first boyfriend (stoner, shaved head, liked extinguishing paper matches on his tongue) when we were driving around on the county roads that stretched out in straight lines from my hometown, bisecting tomato fields. I'd leaned over with the sense of detached curiosity that maybe scientists have when they poke a specimen and think, "How will it react if I do this?" He kept driving, mouth open.

"Interesting," I said, still a scientist.

Polly said, "Never have I ever seen a dead person."

I had never seen a dead person, and neither had Erin.

After he came, my boyfriend pulled over to the side of the road. He encircled me in his arms, kissing every bit of exposed skin between my collar and my ears. "Baby," he said. "Baby, baby, baby." I felt the terrible crush of responsibility. He was horribly tender.

"Never have I ever never kissed an older man," I said.

"I have," said Polly. Erin said nothing, but folded one of her fingers down, laughing.

"You slut!" said Polly.

"But never have I ever done mushrooms!" said Erin.

## CHAPTER 6

There was no insect noise in the woods on Lavender Island. In the summer heat, the wet earth and trees would start to steam, and if you looked closely the blue sky would ripple a bit. But there was none of the generous chirring that I'd expected from such a profusion of vegetable life. The bald eagles mewed some, but mainly because one of our trails went under their nest.

Maureen took me to see the bald eagles while the Floridians were out halibut fishing with Stu, Polly, and Erin. The weather was soft—a light rain that collected in dainty little drops on your hair and sweater fuzz. From the Bake Shop window, I had seen the boat leave from the shore and go out just a little ways. It stayed there for an hour. Then it moved again, and stopped again. Halibut fishing was boring.

Around eleven, I'd seen Maureen crunching up the gravel path, looking over the shoulder of her anorak at the fishing boat rocking gently: a gray boat on gray water. She stood for the moment, hands in pockets, as the boat lurched to life and moved off around the bend of the island. The putt-putt-putt of the engine made its way to us, through the soft weather.

The cookies had just gone in when she came to the open Bake Shop door and knocked solicitously on the particleboard door frame. She also said, "Knock, knock."

"That sure smells good," she said. "Snickerdoodles?" She had written the menu for the week; she knew that snickerdoodles were called for.

"Yes," I said, sparkly. "The same!" The noise of the engine had faded.

"What else do you have to bake?" she asked. She knew, though. She was ceding power to me in an attempt to make me feel like I had my own domain.

"Salmonberry pie for tonight!" Maureen didn't trust me.

"Well," she said, looking around the Bake Shop for signs of uncleanliness: stray rolls of gray flour. "Let's go pick some instead of using the frozen berries for a change. I'll show you the bald eagles' nest."

It was late June. It was not yet the season for salmonberries. I knew this from my aunt. The berries we saw were orange, and the hairs that covered them were fibrous. Maureen walked erect and bent over the bushes with a straight back. She kept looking through the trees at the slice of gray water, looking, probably, for the gray shadow of the boat. But there were too many alders and salmonberry bushes in the way. She led me along the path, carefully weed-whacked at the beginning of the season, toward a peaty outcrop where the alders stopped and the pine trees began. From the tops of one of the tallest pines came the bleating of the eagles.

"We can't get too close," said Maureen, "because the mama eagle will get frantic. But here," she said. "Here's a nice view."

It was a view of the water, and of the rocking boat. Maureen stayed very still and watched it. The figures of the Floridians, and of Stu and Erin, were visible. Polly was inside—setting up sandwiches? Pouring from the thermos of coffee? It was lunchtime—but there was the bright yellow bulk of Stu and the dancing blue figure of Erin. She seemed to be hopping from side to side. The figures separated and went back to helping the guests with their lines, all the guests in their identical orange Grundéns rain gear, the kind real Alaskan fishermen wore.

"The summer I was your age, after high school," said Maureen, "was *the* summer." Maureen's gaze was fixed on the boat; her gray ponytail collected in the hood of her sweatshirt.

"What did you do?" I had been taught that asking questions was polite.

"Mainly drove around at night with my friends. And swam in the pool until my hair turned green," she said. And then, nostalgia gone, the hostess glint in her voice: "You're lucky to be in Alaska. It really is the last frontier. This place molds you."

An excited roar rose off the boat and carried over to us—they were hauling up a halibut. The roar set the eaglets squawking with renewed vigor: they sounded like fully grown songbirds. The mother eagle circled back with her chattering call. Maureen sat with her hands primly capped on her knees. "There will be halibut tonight. Chef will have to batter and fry it—it's best that way."

The blue figure, a little puppet with a tassel on its hat, danced as the yellow figure of Stu lent his strength to hauling up the halibut. When the pale oval of the halibut made its way up through the water, another roar of celebration came off the boat, and the eaglets twittered in agitated response. The blue puppet that was Erin bounced up and threw her arms around yellow Stu.

•

There was a cruel game I played as a young child. It was called "makeover." I would draw someone that I thought was terribly disfigured by bad style or mousiness. Then I'd erase every flaw and add, by scrubbing the edge of my pencil lead against the paper, flourishes of blush and eyeshadow. I think it was less about wishing that more people were beautiful than it was about wishing order on the world: everyone was young and glamorous and thin.

I would do that sometimes when I looked at people, too: I'd think, "Well. All you would have to do is swap out those khakis for a pencil skirt and add some eyeliner, and the hair needs to be longer." When I looked at Maureen, all I thought—again and again, as if it were possible with the right trips to the right stores—was "You need to just be younger. Everything else is fine."

·

I was burning the paper trash as the skiff came in. It was riding low, and Stu, cutting the engine, yelled, "It's a beauty!"

Erin leaped out as soon as the bow scraped the gravel and waved at me with her gloved hands. "Come check it out, Mira!" she said. "Stu says it must be eighty pounds."

The Floridians hoisted the halibut up, and Stu said, "You're our guests! No manual labor for you. Why don't you visit the Beer Creek?"

"Don't have to ask us twice," said a Floridian named Clive.

Polly pushed back the hood of her sweatshirt and slotted her gloved hand into the halibut's gills.

"No," said Stu, "I think I need Erin for this one. You can get the salmon."

Erin and Stu, groaning theatrically for the guests, heaved

the halibut up the beach. Polly returned to the skiff, grabbed the cooler of salmon, and crunched diligently to the fillet table.

Erin was uncool. There was an unfettered buoyancy about her: she had never come to the conclusion that life was there for the scorning. She reeked of a love of paper crafts. Watching Erin's hands adroitly gut a salmon—all the while laughing, and turning pink under the attention of Stu—I could tell that she had wrapped sheets of beeswax around wicks and strung loops of cloth together to make potholders, and had done it with pleasure and pride.

She slid the gutting knife into the salmon's anus without squeamishness and pulled it to its head. She turned the knife and slid it along the inside of the spine, puncturing a thin membrane and scraping out a cylinder of congealed blood. Then, as casually as throwing a Frisbee to a dog, she grabbed the fish by its gills and threw it into the cooler. She looked up at Stu like the rest of us looked up at the mountains, craning back, queasy with the height of it. Stu wasn't even that tall.

·

"I'm just *worried* about her," I heard Polly say, and Stu said, "Yes, you're a good friend. But Erin doesn't seem like a depressed person. Not to me she doesn't. She's doing great here."

I heard this from the footpath; I was taking the trash to the tide line. When my feet hit the beach and the shale started to clatter, Polly and Stu stopped talking. They were the last two people around the dwindling bonfire. Stu was sitting on the gravel, legs spread out, head leaned tipsily back against a log. Polly sat across from him with concerned eyebrows, her chin tucked into the collar of her fleece vest.

"Ahoy there!" said Stu. Polly moved her feet back and forth in the shale chips in the motion you'd use to make the skirt of a snow angel.

"Ahoy," I said. Then the wind shifted and blew smoke into Stu's face, or he just made a show of blinking and coughing as he got to his feet.

"Smoke follows beauty!" said Stu. "Anyway, I'm tucking in. Good night, ladies!"

Polly stayed seated, looking into the coals.

"Polly," I said, "do you want to walk down the beach with me?"

"I'm good," said Polly, and added, "Have you noticed the thing where Stu only likes to talk to one of us at a time?"

"No," I said.

"He has this thing where he only likes to talk to one of us at a time," she said, and she threw a scrap of dry kelp onto the embers.

I had a hard time believing in Polly. If I had known her back home, I would have reserved a hard kernel of resentment for her perfection. But here there was nothing to resent about her at all.

·

I've thought a lot about Stu in the years since Lavender Island. Stu wanted to suckle at his own youth some more, he wanted to be bright-eyed. He wanted what was gone.

I sympathized. When a fishing trawler came chugging past the windows of the Big House, I pressed my hands and nose to the window, making smudges. I'd hold my breath and think, *Crash crash crash*, willing the boat to run aground, discharging a gently wounded Ed.

Because it was my job to wash the windows, I'd later go over all these smudges with a squeaky paper towel and remember the surge I felt looking at the trawler, imagining Ed on the boat with his soft pants and the fake tooth that had most likely replaced the hole in his mouth.

•

The wind picked up sometime during the night. I woke up to the crosshatched sound of spruce branches against the window-pane and thought, "Williwaw!" But it wasn't a williwaw; there was no immediate danger. So I curled up and devoted myself to a problem that had been bothering me—*whether train travel in America was not sleazy, because sleaze needed to be efficient, and whether in that case train travel in Japan was sleazy*—and the needles against the pane became as soothing to me as fingernails scrubbing my scalp.

•

Maureen liked grated carrots in the salad. She liked the lettuce on the sandwiches to be cut into strips. She had an aggressive habit of using two spoons to crush her tea bag, leaching out all of the last tea before throwing it into the compost.

She set herself apart from Erin in this respect. Erin, in the obliviousness of her newfound mastery and dominion over her own body, had no need of exactitude. There was time enough to do things twice, or open up the sandwich and fold a leaf of lettuce back within it. She was delighted enough with the precision of hitting a halibut's skull with a hammer in the correct, exact thunk. All the flowers were blooming just for her. She used the side of her fork to cut up her omelet. Maureen used a knife and fork, gliding over the plate with the practiced squeak of someone who had cut up food for children.

"It's incredible," said Maureen brightly, "how much you're changed—in the little things, mind you—by running a homestead. You get so used to doing everything just so."

The Floridians weren't all that interested in the particulars of homestead life; Maureen was interrupting a recounting of when Clive and Phillipa chartered a boat out of Nassau to fish bonefish. It was the last night of the Floridians' stay, and Erin and Polly had pulled up folding chairs to the dining room table. Erin was eating her fried halibut with her fingers. Malt vinegar or lemon must have gotten into a hangnail; Erin had squawked and was sucking her thumb. Stu kept looking over at her with amazement.

"When we first moved here," Maureen said now, halting the story about the bonefish, "we had no running water, we needed to melt snow. We had buckets and buckets, just standing around. Remember, Stu? Buckets of snow, and a rope of laundry hanging by the wood-burning stove. Our sweaters smelled like wood smoke, even after we got the pipes of the water line in and we could use the taps and run the washing machine off the generator." Stu had turned; he was gesturing at me to bring in more beer.

"Remember that, Stu?" Maureen said. She waved at him. "Earth to Stu! Remember?"

•

After a pancake breakfast, Stu was going to bring the Floridians back to Kodiak. The trip would take all day: they would stop to whale-watch.

Lavender Island felt empty without the Floridians. Erin came into the Bake Shop and sat on the counter, legs jiggling.

"Are you okay?" I asked, giving her a cookie.

"I'm okay," she said. "I guess I'm a little jittery? I can't sleep;

there's so much light. I should ask Stu if there are any blackout curtains."

I went back to my cookie dough. Of course Erin's jittery, I thought. And it has nothing to do with the fact that it never gets dark. There are no ghosts here, and none of Jebediah's demons. There's just an abundance of the kind of sturdy danger that attracts sleaze.

•

When the calendar was flipped to July, there was a sudden blankness. Where there had been cancellations, squares were filled in with white-out. I counted, hopping my finger from one date to the next. Only a few days in July had guests, and several weeks were marked with short lines of yellow highlighter and the letters "S.S."

This stood for Susitna Spirit, a pleasure craft docked in Kodiak. Stu was going to take guests over to the Katmai Peninsula, Maureen told me. A lot of guests these days were in a hurry, she said with the kind of delicacy that indicated she was choosing nice words on purpose. Some guests didn't have the time to experience life on a real homestead, to enjoy Alaskan living. These guests were busy and wanted to see mountains and bears and then go home.

So they were branching out: guided tours on the Susitna Spirit.

"We're trying a few new things," said Maureen, when she saw me looking at the calendar. "And Polly and I will be leading a fly-fishing workshop in Kodiak. The fishing isn't as good in town . . . but we'll keep that our little secret." She took a green highlighter and filled in a few stripes.

"And when Stu is on the Susitna Spirit—he does enjoy being the captain—Erin is going to join him. Those guests do need wrangling, I guess."

•

Later that day, Maureen came into the Bake Shop, big smile. She knocked on the door frame.

"Knock, knock!" she said. I smiled back, rolling up the bag of flour. It was Wednesday afternoon, and there were two salmonberry pies in the oven. There were greased sheets topped with lumps of chocolate chip cookie dough. The pies would start baking at 425, and then I'd turn the oven down to 350. The cookies baked at 350 while the pies were cooling. The bread was shaken out of the loaf pans, already cooling.

"It smells like a dream in here, Mira! You're so lucky to get these smells instead of fish gurry." She clasped her hands. "Well, *we're* the lucky ones, that you're here."

"Thanks so much!"

"And, Mira—oh!—it's so tidy in here. Really shipshape. You've really got the knack of it."

"Thanks so much!"

"But I'm not just here to tell you how much we love your talents. The thing is—well, food generally costs more in Alaska than in the lower forty-eight, and then it's extra to bring supplies in from town. We really have to watch every penny, and I noticed we've been spending a bit on baking supplies, actually a little more than in years past."

I had chocolate chips in my pocket; my breakfast had been cookie dough and grated coconut.

"Now, I know how tempting it is to snitch," Maureen said. "And Lord knows that cookie dough is even better than freshly baked cookies. But I need to ask you to be extra vigilant, because this stuff is *costly*. We're getting it shipped in, and even in bulk, well—we're trying to keep the overhead down."

"I understand. I'm sorry."

Maureen threw her head back. "No need to be sorry—like I said, who doesn't love cookie dough?" I tugged at the elastic waistband of my chef pants. Maureen clasped her hands again. "In any case, we're going to have a bit of a relaxing time of it throughout July. So!" She looked around. "How are things looking? Do we have enough supplies to get us through to August?"

"I think we'll need more chocolate chips and coconut," I said.

"Really? Already? That doesn't seem right." She opened the drawers and took out the big bag of chocolate chips. It was almost empty.

"And we're out of marshmallows," I said. The marshmallows were kept in the Bake Shop; the other s'mores fixings were kept in the Big House pantry. Sometimes I played Chubby Bunny—how many marshmallows can you fit in your mouth and still manage to say the words "Chubby Bunny"?—by myself.

"Mira," said Maureen. "We can't have this."

.

Chef cross-checked his shopping list with the shopping list of the Bake Shop.

"Not enough eggs," he said, stabbing his finger at the paper. "Not enough eggs or butter or onions—"

"Oh, Chef," said Maureen, taking the list from him, "we're going to be doing more fishing excursions in town, and more outings on the Susitna Spirit. You'll have time to relax!"

When she left, Chef said, "This doesn't seem right. Back at Mercury River Camp, we went through that amount of butter in a day."

•

One of the lessons of the frontier was that there was no holiday without the balance of exertion beforehand. According to the *Farmers' Almanac*, the Fourth of July was to be a bluebird day. We were going to go on a picnic. There was a lot of work to be done.

On the third of July, everyone in the Big House woke up early to the smell of bacon frying and the sound of Maureen's house shoes clopping around. Maureen was frying the bacon; Chef deserved a lie-in. Maureen had her glasses on and a yellow legal pad. She was wearing her most authoritative fleece vest. She was not interested in dallying; she sipped her coffee in a way that showed everyone how eager she was to be alert.

"Where's Stu?" asked Polly.

"He's up checking the water line for leaks and blockages," said Maureen. "Erin, Stu wants your help. After the water line, you can mow the lawn."

"But I usually check the water line," said Polly.

"Polly," Maureen said, "you're going to help me in the gear shed first. We need to give it a good tidying. After that, we're going into the garden. Mira, we need to fix the cabins for our next guests. Give them a nice deep clean. All the nooks and crannies. Unfortunately, one of our guests seems to have left chewing gum stuck on the doorknobs of Guest Cabins Three and Four; we need to clean that off. Then we're going to need desserts for tomorrow, because it isn't the Fourth of July without strawberry shortcake and apple pie.

"These are our projects," she said, ticking something on the yellow pad. "We're going to have to work extra today, because tomorrow is our picnic. The weather is supposed to be magnificent."

. . .

I had cleaned the cabins after the Floridians had left, given them a thorough vacuuming and dusting. They smelled strongly of the fresh pine potpourri I'd left in the drawers. But this time, Maureen said, it would be good to go over the floors with orange oil. The lapse between guests would allow enough time for the oil to dry completely. I vacuumed the floors again; there was always ash kicked up from the topsoil, left over from the Novorupta eruption of 1912. On my hands and knees, I was Cinderella, like every girl scrubbing floors.

I came to a new conclusion about sleaze, right there on the floor: sleaze required the domestic as much as it needed danger. In fact, I thought, as I tied up my hair in a kerchief, domesticity was arguably even more vital to the existence of sleaze. After all, without immediate danger, sleaze can create its own danger—it can metabolize itself and—*poof*—danger is there. But sleaze isn't sleazy until it's judged and reprimanded. It needs a tether.

The ideal location, then, to attract sleaze was in proximity to danger and the honeytrap of domesticity. And I congratulated myself on—this time around, at least—getting it right. I lived adjacent to a volcano, I could put hospital corners on a guest bed, and my pies really were getting to be quite excellent.

·

Mid-morning on the Fourth of July, we all piled into the skiff and took our picnic to a white rock beach on the Shelikof side of Tugidak Island. The Shelikof Strait was a dangerous stretch of water, Stu had said. But on a bluebird day it was serene, reflecting little round clouds and the mountains of the Katmai Peninsula.

We sat in a circle, all of us, on the white stone beach. We roasted hot dogs over a fire that Stu made, and ate the strawberry shortcake. Both Maureen and Stu had their best host voices on; the rest of us were chipper, ready for guests with no guests in sight.

Stu told jokes, intentionally bad and intentionally family-friendly—*What do you call a fish with no eye? Fsh.* Erin did handstands in the white pebbles. After lunch, Chef wandered away down the beach, where he grew smaller and skinnier until he was the height and width of a match.

After Maureen had curled up with a book and Stu had lain

down, Polly stretched out on a log with her pants rolled up and her shirt tucked into her bra. She already had the expression she'd carry on her face for the rest of the summer. I was standing no more than a yard away from her, but she looked at me like her eyes were focusing on the mountains across the Shelikof Strait.

"Where are you going?" she asked.

I walked the opposite direction down the beach from Chef. The waters of the Shelikof beached a lot of marine trash. I found, among the usual bleached orange buoys and the gnarls of fishing twine, a Febreze bottle, a purple bucket, and a Lego hat.

I walked as far as a small stream. It was idyllic, with its burbling and small floats of foamy algae, and the thrashing movement of salmon backs. I had the childish thought of making my home here forever and ever and ever. The stream arced into the forest; a group of puffins flapped across the water. I had to sit down, because something about the scene—little budding flowers and tight blue sky—produced a feeling of immensity in me that was like fear. The light was so bright. The campfire smoke rose in a vertical column. I was the only human I could hear.

There was nothing to stop me from thinking of my aunt just then. No domesticity, no danger, no hope of sleaze in the immediate vicinity, nothing that Ed might have touched. I lay down with my cheek on the warm rocks of the beach, back to the water, face pointed up toward the mountains. For a last sight of the world, this seemed like a good one, even if she had seen it in the cold of October with Sammy from Sammy's Air shouting in the background.

When I came back, Erin was doing aerobics and Stu was watching her with his hands lying on his belly in a satisfied way. Maureen was looking at Stu. Polly was still lying on the log, looking at Maureen. I was looking at all of them, and Chef, still tiny, still walking away down the beach without fear, was looking across the water at the Aleutian Range.

.

When we returned to Lavender Island and were unloading the picnic boxes and the coolers—the ride back had been silent, the noise of the motor making it unnecessary to talk—we heard the low drone of a skiff.

"Goodness," said Maureen. "The Lawson clan."

In a little inlet on neighboring Tugidak Island, obscured from the passage of the fishing boats and tenders, there was another homestead. "Newcomers," Maureen called them.

They'd secured their homestead in the eighties—they hadn't gone through the hallowed procedures of the Homestead Act, they hadn't gotten their land for free in exchange for five years of hard work domesticating their plot. They had used money from wealthy Idaho parents to make a godly life on Kodiak, away from even the harmless earthly temptations of Coeur d'Alene.

The Lawson clan was a true clan. Young Maggie and Steven Lawson had spent the first two summers building up their homestead and the following years having babies. There were seven children; all were instructed at home in the basics of fishing, carpentry, and the Scripture.

They were all alike, all towheaded and virtuous-looking, and I was a little afraid of them—there were so many of the same child. Some were girls and some were boys, but they all wore the same Alaskan uniform of soft pants, a hoodie, and a fleece vest. The father jumped onto the beach, a big rack of Budweiser in his arms, and the children obediently dragged the skiff up to high ground.

"Happy Fourth of July!" crowed Mr. Steven Lawson, dropping the rack of Budweiser. Two children scampered to open it and put the Budweiser in the Beer Creek. He gave Maureen a big hug, and he gave Stu a firm handshake. Maggie Lawson gave everyone a wave.

"Well, now that you've brought over the King of Beers," said Stu, "you might as well stay for dinner."

"That's what we thought!" said Steven Lawson, and opened a backpack that was full of hot dogs and buns and sparklers.

The Lawson children were true children of the frontier. They found firewood and twisted little cones of paper to make the kindling more flammable. The smaller ones disappeared into the underbrush to find sticks for the weenie roast. I went into the Bake Shop and came back with the apple pies, which I set on a card table that had materialized from out of nowhere. The dachshunds wriggled underfoot and begged for bits of hot dog.

"You girls," said Stu conspiratorially, "you can have beer. It's the Fourth of July. But no more than two." We brought back big armfuls of cans from the Beer Creek, for the adults, for each of us girls, and for the oldest sons of the Lawson clan, who were fourteen or fifteen but behaved, alternately, as if they were fifty or five.

"The weather has been very mild this summer," said one of the Lawson boys.

"We went octopus fishing the other day and got a real big one. It looked like snot," said the other. He high-fived his brother.

Before we were given a hot dog to spear on a stick, the Lawson clan all joined hands. We joined hands, too. "God is great and God is good, and we thank Him for this food," they chanted in unison. "By His hand we are all fed, give us, Lord, our daily bread." When we dropped hands and lifted our bowed heads, Maureen had the belladonna eyes and girlish flush that I'd later learn to associate with the grateful look someone gives you after you slap them.

The Lawson clan was a machine; they knew exactly how to roast a weenie so it didn't char. Even the smallest children seemed to know how to handle their sticks, scraping at them dutifully with Swiss Army knives until they were sharp. In fact, it was one of the younger ones, a girl about seven, who announced solemnly that the tide was going out and they should go soon—they didn't want to have to push the bottom of the skiff over too many feet of shale beach.

With two Budweisers in me, I felt a great welling of affection for everyone on the beach. The Lawson clan I studied with the condescending fascination of the well-meaning tourist. They all wore identical Xtratuf boots, in various sizes. The small boots were so cute; the children that I would conceive with Ed would wear tiny Xtratufs. And they had *done* it, man. They had lived in the grace of God in a compound surrounded by Sitka spruce. Stu was a bon viveur, ruddy and chuckling. He really should go to town more and be around people he could be jocular with. Maureen was holy—she should go to town more and go worship. Erin was the nicest sort of imbecile—she was asking the Lawson boys about fishing for octopus and saying, "With *bleach*? Isn't that bad for the environment?" No one cared about the environment; there was too much of it in Alaska. And Polly was destined for such happiness by virtue of her beauty: only the most wholesome of men would please her, only the most wholesome men would be truly pleased with her princess looks. Even Chef—who had run off to his tent cabin as soon as the twin skiffs arrived around the spit, motoring toward us with such speed—he was okay. I wished him a nice death.

As the Lawsons' skiffs disappeared, Erin broke out in tipsy, ratcheting sobs. Maureen stood up from her seat on the log, but Stu was already over by her. His face was as pink as a ham from the sun and the beer.

"What's wrong, now? Now, what's wrong?"

"They kill the octopus with bleach. With *bleach*."

"There, there. A little bleach never hurt anything. In fact, people use bleach to clean out aquariums all the time. The bleach just scares the little guys out of their hiding spots, and then you kill them very quickly, like a halibut." His hand circled Erin's waist. "Very quickly."

·

The obituary for Stu, some ten years later, read simply: he was outlived by his twin sons, both residents of Fairbanks, he was a man who loved the water and the mountains alike, and he was one of the last homesteaders. There was no mention of Erin, except in the phrase "He will be sorely missed."

By that point, Erin was in Hawaii. Her Facebook profile picture showed a woman almost ropy with strength, like a ballerina. Her hair was still dyed red, her smile was still wide, and she was wearing a sensible two-piece bathing suit on a Hawaiian beach, surfboard under her arm. Under her clavicle, she'd gotten a tattoo of what looked like a sprig of fireweed. I had never friended her, but occasionally I'd find her page anyway and look at what I could. There: she had bought a parrot.

CHAPTER 7

In the second week of July, Erin and Stu left for Kodiak.
They were picking up guests from town and taking them directly
to tour Katmai on board the Susitna Spirit. The morning they
left, Polly came into the Bake Shop.

"Can I have one?" She pointed to the lumps of chocolate chip
cookie dough on the buttered sheet.

"Maureen said no eating cookie dough," I said. "We have to
conserve."

"Maureen's a fucking cunt," said Polly, and she took a bite of one. "This place," she said, speaking through the dough, "was different last year. There were seven employees. The chef was, like, a nice fat woman from Utah."

A seiner moved past the point. I watched it, hoping it would run aground. Polly watched it, too, eating another raw cookie.

"Want to know a secret? Did you know that Erin and Stu are going to share a bedroom on the Susitna Spirit? Erin told me," said Polly. "Don't tell Maureen, I guess. I guess Maureen doesn't know. Erin said it was practical. She said, *did I think the guests would mind?*"

Originally, the plan had been for Stu to sleep on a sofa bed, Polly told me, but it was decided that was impractical—what if one of the guests wanted to get up early, fix some coffee, and have a bit of silent meditation? So Erin and Stu were sharing one of the rooms with bunk beds.

"There are plenty of beds," said Polly. "There is a single bed, and there's a double bed. *Two* sofa beds."

I didn't know what to say, so I just offered Polly another raw cookie. She laughed, and then said, "Whatever. Whatever, right? In a few months, I'll be backpacking through Southeast Asia. I've decided."

She had a deferred field-hockey scholarship. She launched into a boring story about field hockey and away games. Her memories were very sunny—practices on long September afternoons, trips in a big bus to a neighboring town, group pictures where everyone jumped at once. It's one of the world's oldest sports, she said. Her sweatshirt had a design of an elephant holding a field-hockey stick with its trunk.

"Did you play a sport?" said Polly, and I felt both the sadness of not being part of Polly's glossy coterie and the sadness of Polly's sadness.

"No," I said. And then, "Sorry."

"That's okay," said Polly. And then, "I don't know. I just think the sharing a bedroom thing on the Susitna Spirit is not cool."

It would probably be a tussle, I thought. I played it out like a vignette of me and Ed: Stu claims the bottom bunk usually, but one night, Erin plonks down in the bottom bunk. Get out of there, says Stu. Nope, says Erin, I'm staying. That's mine, says Stu, and he runs his hand through his hair so it's standing on end. Take the other bunk, says Erin, and she turns over and curls up.

The captain gets that bunk, says Ed, and I roll back over. Oh? I say. The *captain* gets this bunk? That's right, says Ed. What are you going to do about it, then? What am I going to do about it? says Ed. He's been chewing his bottom lip. All right, he says, you asked for it.

"What are you looking at?" asked Polly. My eyes had been unfocused, pointed in the direction of the bowl of cookie dough.

"You know what I'd do if I were you," said Polly, pointing at the cookie dough. "I'd spit in that."

"Oh no," I said. "Oh, I wouldn't."

"Or pour in some ipecac," said Polly.

•

What Polly said about the number of beds on the Susitna Spirit reminded me of something I was told in elementary school during a sleepover. It was a sex story, and remains to this day one of the most titillating I've ever heard. A girl—she later became sleazy, forever sucking on Dimetapp bear-shaped lollipops—was telling us about the torrid affair that she imagined being conducted between our teachers, Ms. Green and Mr. Hodge.

"Mr. Hodge likes Ms. Green, and he decides to invite her over to his house. Ms. Green decides that she wants to, so she goes out and buys a new dress—a new *red* dress—and gets a manicure. She walks up to his front door. He answers the door. They go into the living room, where there's no sofa. There's no TV. There's no chairs. There's a *bed*. They go into the dining room, where there's a *bed*. The hall has a skinny little *bed* in it. In his study there's a *bed*. In the kitchen there's a *bed*. In his bedroom there's a huge *bed* that takes up most of the room. In the den there's a *bed*. In the family room there's a *bed*. And in the backyard there's a—"

We were waiting, almost drooling. "There's a *hammock*."

·

The next day, the tender came to deliver groceries and left Claire behind with us.

I didn't know about Claire before she arrived. There was no "Claire!" on the calendar. A nine-year-old child was just off-loaded in the same manner that the new groceries were off-loaded. She was standing on the beach among the boxes, saying nothing, as we hefted the groceries up to the stairs. She didn't offer to help. She just stood and looked down, with her hair hanging in front of her face. When she raised her head, I could see that she had been sucking a strand of it. She spit it out when I looked at her.

She did that often: she sucked her hair and then waited until it had dried and was crispy and then worried the little spikes of it with her fingers. In the night, I could hear her do it, a little scuffling sound like mice in the ceiling. I could hear her do it because, as it turned out, she was to sleep in my bedroom.

When we were hauling the boxes, Maureen said, "Mira, meet Claire." I put down the box.

"Hey, Claire." I stuck out my hand, but that was not the correct way to greet a little girl. Maureen looked at me warmly. This was a lesson.

"This is our guest, Claire," said Maureen. "She'll be sharing your bedroom."

It was impossible to be snippy. I was older than Claire, and Claire was a guest, and Polly and Erin already shared a room. I couldn't say anything but "Oh!" and make my face into a smile.

The girl looked up at me with an unimpressed look. I was, it's true, unimpressive. There was batter in the weave of my corduroy pants.

"Why don't you," said Maureen, with the kind of smile in her voice that you wear for telephone conversations, "take Claire's things and get her settled in. We'll take care of everything else."

I had no choice but to heft the girl's little duffel and say, in a voice that was attempting to be heave-ho, "Come on, Claire!"

Claire dawdled. Once out of Maureen's sight, she lost her woebegone look but stopped being able to move quickly. The first thing she did when we had gone up the steps and were hidden by the alders was to spy the beer cooling in the stream.

"Why are those there?" she asked.

"To cool," I said.

"To *drink*?" she asked. "Do you drink those?"

I had only had two, in quick succession, on the Fourth of July. But I said, in an attempt to make this child enamored of me, "I do. I do drink those."

I heard that I was trying to sound grown-up, and so did she. She took the note of pride in my voice as solidarity, and said, "I've gotten drunk. I've gotten drunk on Jack Daniel's and milk."

I didn't laugh, because the first time I had gotten drunk I had mixed vanilla extract and pineapple extract and banana extract together and put it in an old crystal decanter and felt like a real lady.

"Were you sick?" I asked Claire.

"No," Claire said. "I was dizzy."

My room was not the kind of place where a little girl would be happy. There was nothing pretty about it. There were two beds, both of which I slept in, because I was fitful for change and thought that waking up on two sides of the same room would give it to me faster. I had recently started sleeping more in the right-hand bed, for no particular reason. Left open, on this bed, was a copy of the Kodiak phone book. I moved it quickly.

"Who were you going to call?" asked Claire.

I had no immediate answer to that. I couldn't call anyone, because we weren't allowed to use the expensive satellite phone.

I had the phone book there because I had a habit of looking up Ed's name and number. There he was, between S. Gaill and Lorna Gall. He lived on a cul-de-sac, in an apartment complex. These were things I had recently discovered.

I had started by standing in the office, which wasn't a separate room at all and was just a little nook at the end of the upstairs opposite the staircase, and flipping idly through the phone book until I had found his name. This process, the unhurried casualness of searching and finding his name, was exciting. I panted.

In the same way I meted out all pleasure that summer, I looked forward to the time when I would do this.

First it was in the mid-afternoon, when no one was around. I stood in a way that suggested I was so bored I was just reading through the phone book, just for fun. But that wasn't exciting enough. I started looking up Ed's name in the evening, when Erin or Polly could walk by at any moment. This was so thrilling I had to sit down and cross my legs vigorously or rush into my room and masturbate. Once, even, Polly walked by. But this turned out to be a huge deflation: she didn't say, "Who are you lusting after? I can see it blazing in your eyes," and I didn't have to confess. She just walked by, nodded, and lay facedown on her bed with her bedroom door still open. That had the effect of turning the act of looking up Ed's name in the open into something dull.

So I started taking the phone book into my room. This added a dimension—in the privacy of my room, I found that there was a street map of Kodiak in the back of the phone book, and I could see where Ed lived. The apartment complex was near the Walmart. It was up the mountain rather than close to shore. But even that game became stale, although I still got a spasm of pleasure every time I saw his little name on that thin white paper.

It wasn't until Claire asked who I was going to call that I thought of actually calling him, of him picking up the phone, of him saying something in that voice, which was a little pinched and reedy, like, I thought, his voice was cracking in sexual anguish.

"I'm not going to call anyone," I said to Claire. "I was just looking at the map of Kodiak."

"I'll show you where I live," said Claire, and sat down cross-legged on what was now her bed.

.

During the day, Claire followed me about wherever I went. This wasn't her fault.

Maureen took me aside in the sunroom after Claire had gone to bed. It was eleven o'clock at night, and the sky was still a nice pearly color, like midday during a rainstorm. She sat down on one of the rockers and reached over and patted the other rocker so that it swung back and forth.

"I got this chair when the twins were babies," she said. I thought she might try some sort of maternal angle; here it was.

Her face as she looked over the slope with the vegetable garden was gentle. The long civil twilight was doing a good job at making her pretty. Her hair looked silvery and almost blond, her eyes were downcast, and she did look motherly: full of worry and aching happiness. She folded her hands in her lap.

"Claire is one of the less fortunate girls in Kodiak," said Maureen. "I've been working with a few of these girls each summer. Their parents are often drunk or on methamphetamine. Claire's father was a crabber in the Bering Sea, and he drowned. That's a horrible death. And, the way a lot of crabbers live, at least when they're young, he didn't put any money aside. Her mother works at Katmai Dry Goods."

I didn't know what to say. Ed would put money aside for me; I would never end up working at Katmai Dry Goods. I was looking for what Maureen might want me to say about this, but Maureen just looked at her folded hands in the gray light.

"Her mother works hard. But Claire doesn't have the life that a lot of children have in Kodiak. Kodiak's very much about money—who has it, who doesn't. It's good for her to come to a place like this, somewhere remote."

She paused to look out to sea. It was very easy to make everything sound sorrowful, I thought, when you could just turn and stare out at an expanse of cold water that would kill you in fifteen minutes.

"This place can really help girls come into their own. I offered to have her come out here for a while and benefit from homestead life. To interact with hardworking young women, like you. She'll probably want to spend a lot of time with you. Show her the magic you work in the Bake Shop. Take her on walks. Polly and I will take her fishing, of course, but you'll want to be her special friend."

You could not say "special friend" and get away with it, even when you were looking onto the gray mirrored surface of the water. I rocked a little harder in my rocking chair. But I think Maureen took that for a vigorousness in my maternal constitution. She gave me a smile, as if to say that all was right with the world. Then she went and stood at one of the panes of the sunroom with her hands folded behind her back.

"We must do all we can to help others," she said. "The smallest things have a lasting impact on children."

This was absurd. I was rocking now angrily enough to give a squeak every time the rocker reached the top of its curve and began its descent. Maureen was silhouetted against the green hills and gray sky.

Maybe, I thought later, Maureen hadn't been being manipulative. Maybe she had been being earnest. That was a thought that made me feel bad for her.

.

The Jenkins twins were in Fairbanks. That's where Maureen ended up; leading tours out on the Chena River in the summer and Northern Lights viewings in the winter. Her picture on the tour company's website was her grinning, wearing a snowsuit, arms thrown wide. That's what I know for sure.

What I imagine is this: With alimony and a steady paycheck, she was able to buy a small house in a subdevelopment. The living room window would look out onto the street—in the winter, the haloes of streetlamps and the vaguely underwater movements of the snowplow moving down the road—but the kitchen and the bedroom looked out onto the backyard, which had no back fence and instead seamlessly ran into a small forest that contained, among the firs, birch trees. For that reason, I assume

Maureen didn't spend much time in the living room, and the sofa and armchair set she'd bought on layaway, and paid back diligently and promptly, remained almost untouched.

Instead, she sat at the kitchen table, which she bought new but which soon acquired the comforting finish of coffee rings and the smooth discoloration brought on by hot serving bowls and plates. If she needed to feel cozy—for example, when she had a slight head cold—she read in bed. She bought a TV, intending it for the living room, but set it up atop her chest of drawers so she could watch it from a position propped up by pillows.

In early 2004, she surprised herself by getting an HBO subscription. She became enraptured. In the evening, she'd watch a show, and then, in the morning, looking at the deer tracks on the fresh snow in the backyard, leading into the naked birches, she'd think back on everything that had occurred in the show the night before. It gave her an itchy restlessness—there were places she'd never go and sorts of people she'd never be among—which left her in the same calm way a headache fades; all that remained was a peaceful understanding that she had made the correct decisions in life. There were so many mistakes she had not made, mistakes that were only possible, it seemed, in places like New Jersey and Baltimore.

Then she'd call one of the ladies from her women's prayer group. The snow was thick, but maybe they'd want to join her at the community pool. There was nothing like swimming a few laps to feel like it was summer again.

·

I had to enter my room silently, turning the knob before I closed the door. The room was full of the warm smell of sleep—a clean, almost milky smell, because Claire was still a child. I stood on the bed and silently propped the window open.

Claire didn't even move. She slept on her back with her arms flung wide. The Kodiak phone book was on the nightstand near her bed, but I thought it would be too risky to reach over and get it and flip through the soft pages until I got to Ed's name. She might wake up and want to talk.

·

In fact, though, she had to wake me. I slept cozily in the nest of our shared body heat under that slanted roof. She was already dressed and sitting on the edge of her bed when I woke.

"Good morning!" I said heartily, and then, when she turned and I saw that her expression was grateful, I realized that she would expect me to be hearty from then on.

It was a slow wake-up. Maureen had given us permission to sleep in, and we were still fumbling to refill the coffeepot at eight. The fact that the coffeepot had been filled and drained once meant that Chef was up and had probably eaten and gone back to bed, or gone to sit in the sun with his feet in the water. I hoped, for Claire's sake, that his shirt wasn't off.

This was one of the first times I had been around a child once they had stopped being filthy but hadn't yet become sweaty with adolescence. Claire's hair wasn't perfectly brushed, but it shone. She had an embarrassing milk mustache when she lifted up her cereal bowl to drink the last spoonfuls, but she scrubbed it off with a napkin.

Nine was hard for me to remember, and maybe that's why I thought of her as being such a clean little thing. At nine, the searing emotions brought on by sudden unnameable fears, the feverish play that bled into my real life, had eroded. That was early childhood: a horrible incessant murmur within my head, and the constant logical structure of the world outside, and the deep discomfort when they collided—a fan in an open window brought in the cool night air, but I believed that it also brought in nightmares, and because of this I dissolved into silent tears when I was put to bed in the summertime.

Then, by ten, I was already concerned with adulthood. I looked up the dictionary definitions for sexy, unknowable terms: "orgasm," "refractory period." But nine? Nine was clean. Nine was in an air-conditioned aisle at the drugstore, picking out school supplies.

Claire trained her eyes on me and asked what we were going to do today. Maureen interrupted, "It's a bluebird day. Why don't you take a walk?"

Claire nodded. She did not seem to be interested in walking, but that's what Maureen had suggested and that's what we did. I strode, and Claire was soon darting back and forth from picking something or other off the ground and seeing something in the grass.

"When does school start?" I said, eventually.

"August 31," she said, chirping. She picked up a stick and then threw it humming into the long grass.

I didn't want to ask if she was excited, so I asked her, "Are you sad?"

"Sad?"

"That school's starting so soon?"

"No!" she said, sending another stick humming. "It's so far away."

It was July. August was so far away. She would have several more summers before this one was over.

I had no idea what else to ask her, so we walked on. Finally, she said, "Do you have a boyfriend?"

"No," I said, and she asked, "Are you in love?" and I said, honestly, "Very much so."

"Who is he?" she asked, and I said, "His name is Ed."

•

I had always thought that the ideal man's name is only one syllable long. Ed proved this. It's not that I believed that brevity was a measure of masculinity. Daniel Day-Lewis, for example, especially Daniel Day-Lewis in *The Last of the Mohicans*, was very masculine and had a multisyllabic name.

But you can't manage more than one syllable at the point of orgasm without forethought. You open your mouth and a syllable is strangled out: "Unh" or "Yes" or "Fuck" or "Ed." Only with a little extra thinking can you manage the name "Daniel Day-Lewis" or even "Daniel." It's that extra thinking that turns the moment from passion to passion tinged with artifice.

I had been told that orgasming to the thought of someone bound you to that person forever. I think I read this in a well-meaning text for adolescent girls (a magazine, maybe, or a Health class pamphlet). The purpose of this dubious fact was to ward adolescent girls away from promiscuity, but whoever wrote it was a fool. There was nothing to me, as an adolescent girl, that was more alluring than the idea of being bound in some secret and illicit way to another person forever.

I remember waking up from a sex dream starring Daniel Day-Lewis (from *The Last of the Mohicans*) and thinking, "We're bound together forever." In a kind of frenzied alchemy, I would chant the names of whoever I fantasized about, whoever I wanted to be bound to, as I came.

But it's always been the single-syllable names that have come out of my mouth without provocation. Therefore, I believed that there were two kinds of men: men with one-syllable names know that their names are being squealed in a moment of ecstasy without pretense, and men with long names know that their names come out of the mouths of their partners after careful, loving forethought. It was easier, of course, for a man with a one-syllable name to be sleazy.

.

Claire and I walked to the bald eagles' nest, and they started shrieking, and the mother kept flapping around. I thought Claire would be awed. But she just kept picking up sticks and throwing them into the bushes.

"Bald eagles," I suggested.

"Yeah," she said. Near the nest, the woods were very dense and green, and the stumps were covered in moss. "They're a nuisance over at Walmart," she said. "And the dumpster by my house. They always fight over fish."

"Look," I said. "What do you want to do?"

"I'm not sure," she said. "I thought it would be different out here, but it's exactly the same."

We walked down to a little beach full of rocks and snarled with driftwood. She looked around. She toed a rock, stepping away when a white little grub underneath it flipped into a crawl. There was nothing she found remarkable about any of it. It really was a boring little beach—it would have been nice if there had been waves, but there was only the steady lap lap of the water against the shore.

I did the only thing I could think of, which was to take her into the Bake Shop. We passed Chef on the way there; he was walking back from the beach on his dwindling matchstick legs.

"He's Chef," I said to Claire, and she didn't seem to register that there was anything strange about him. He might have been like a bald eagle in that respect. I began to think that Maureen had been around tourists too long, and now she thought of Kodiak as a metropolis, full of gravel lots and without bald eagles stamping the sky above the Walmart and in the open dumpsters, and without men like Chef stalking around smoothing the sides of their mustaches.

Claire wanted to make snickerdoodles, which were the easiest cookie to make. Something about this fact—snickerdoodles seemed sort of dumb and helpless—and something about their name, and about Claire's eagerness, made me deeply sad.

Claire needed help figuring out which one the teaspoon was.

She didn't know how to cream butter and sugar. With Claire around, there was no time to watch my future with Ed projected on the blank Bake Shop wall.

Claire seemed, on the whole, like a snickerdoodle. She smelled a little like a baked good. There was a rasp in her voice like burnt sugar. But it was her impossible youth—I was very old at eighteen—and the evidences of her stupidity that made her really helpless in my mind. Of course, she might have been bright. I had no idea. It was impossible to extricate the two things—childhood and idiocy—and I got them confused.

·

Stu and Erin came back from their first Susitna Spirit trip on the same day that Polly and Maureen went out to Kodiak to teach the fly-fishing camp. There was barely a spoken exchange: just the rustle of boxes and duffels and the clank of the skiff bottom against the gravel of the beach. I sat on the steps and watched with Claire as Stu stepped out of the skiff, Erin bounded, and Polly and Maureen trotted brightly down the beach.

When Chef cooked on cold evenings or mornings, the bay

windows of the dining room fogged. I thought of this as a greasy fog, but that's just because the food was oily, and because whenever the windows grew foggy smeared traces from fingers or noses appeared.

Chef was at the stove. Erin was in the shower. Claire was sitting in front of the TV, watching *Freaky Friday*. I found Stu when I went in to set the table; he was sitting at his usual place by the door, drinking. His face was flushed from alcohol and salt and sun. Oh, I thought. He's handsome.

Stu wore the same loose woolly pants as everyone else in Kodiak; he walked with a seaman's roll, like Ed. There was something of the sea about him, that unsteadiness and loneliness. He had both hands around a Mason jar full of wine. Erin's singing was coming from the bathroom, and there were onions in half an inch of oil on the stove.

When Erin emerged, with her hair stamped wetly to her forehead and cheeks, Stu looked up with a big, dazed smile.

It was a quiet meal. We had turned off the TV before Claire had finished *Freaky Friday*, and she kept shifting in her seat with the anxiety of someone who's been woken up mid-dream. Chef was uncharacteristically silent, unused to sitting with Stu at mealtimes. The food was soft and made no noise as we ate it.

Erin was silent and glowing. Stu was silent and glancing up at Erin with his reddened face—every look of his increased her glowing, which caused him to duck his head down to his Mason jar and drink more wine, which caused him to look up at her again.

Erin's beautiful future was being created in brilliant colors. She didn't have to wait until November. Erin had no need to watch and re-watch her beautiful future, because it was there and it was happening, and she sang in the shower under the hot water and the influence of that grapefruit soap.

·

Then it was time for me to do the dishes, with Claire's incessant help. She cleared the table with the weird methodical nature of all children. I watched through the kitchen window as Chef walked back to his tent cabin in the twilight. Chef was a silhouette, his limbs burnt matchsticks. The alders still rustled silver. It was mid-July, and the days were getting shorter. The air turned blue around ten, flickering into darkness at midnight and dawning with churning birdsong by three.

Between the progression of the plates into the kitchen and the progression of the glasses, I saw a shudder in the blue patch of grass between the Guest Cabins. It was Stu, swaying a little and then sitting in one of the Adirondack chairs. There was another shudder, and a shape detached itself from the darker blue of the trees. That was Erin. She hopped into a bobbing lunge, or maybe a curtsy. Stu got to his feet and walked toward Erin, and then I had to turn around, because there was Claire with a bouquet of forks, asking where they should go. I told her she could finish *Freaky Friday,* because it meant I could finish the dishes and walk the garbage down to the tide line alone.

When I turned back, the twilight had become one shade darker, and I was aware of my own face bobbing up toward the surface of the windowpane. I couldn't see Stu or Erin anywhere.

Outside, it was hard to tell whether the air was actually colder or if the night was just darker. Where the waves splashed back there was a play of luminescent plankton, glinting like the water at midday. When I got to the end of the beach, I checked the shadows for the shadows of bears and sat in a heap on the shale and watched the plankton. They made me uneasy, and not just because they were glowing unnaturally in a blue world. The phosphorescence was just strange enough that it was hard not to imagine that this was one of those blurry interim images you see before you start dreaming—the time when your pleasant fantasies (Ed, unzipping his pants) twist into strangeness (Ed's cock, winding like a vine down his leg) and you acknowledge with an opiated surrender that this is the beginning of sleep. I sat there on the shale, in an astronomical twilight that may have been cold or may just have been dark, staring at plankton that seemed, to me, to be heralding a good eight hours of sleep.

There was a scrabbling sound, something moving along the upper edge of the shale. In the mist rising near the silvery alders was a dogged little shape. I thought it was a bear cub until I heard my name and realized it was Claire.

"What are you doing?" I asked.

"It's Erin," she said. "Erin's missing."

"What do you mean?"

"Stu came into the Big House and asked if I'd seen Erin. I hadn't, and then Stu checked and she's not in her room, either. She's gone."

We walked along the beach, and I wondered if I should hold her hand. Where could Erin have gone?

"Stu doesn't know. He's worried."

It struck me then how dangerous this was. The nearest town with a hospital was four hours away by boat. The Lawson clan, way over on Tugidak, would be asleep by now. There were five people in the camp: one was missing, one was drunk, one was feeble, one was a child, and one was me. We were outnumbered by bears. Bears were not charming. The water was not charming. The mist in the alders wasn't charming. The plankton glimmered angrily.

But Claire marched along. She was happy. I said, "Don't be scared," and she answered, "This is exciting."

And, of course, it was exciting. The lowered light was like Halloween. There was a missing person! Claire's face in the gloom, a little clean plate.

When I had been smaller and didn't have crushes on men who liked danger, I'd had a crush on danger. It was the menace itself that was so tantalizing.

I had liked, particularly, the idea of a diffuse threat. The phrase I would repeat to myself, repeating myself into a reverie, was "It's coming." Or, softer, spoken under a blanket, "They're coming." The "to get me" was implied. When I said it often enough, I was lulled by the music of it, and the world turned demented at my will. "It's coming," and the fluttering of the bedroom curtain was horrific. "It's coming," and the fan set in the window to cool the house was whirring with intent, sending out signals. "It's coming," and the chorus of the cicadas was chopped into Morse code.

When I was older and had consumed enough literature where the girls who died were the pious, uninteresting ones so that I equated death with blandness, I became the survivor in my fantasies. I thought about holding sacks of grain and running through the snow barefoot. I was in charge of taking care, of bringing the young orphans close, all heavy and damp. I preserved the innocence of youth.

To this end, I put my arm cautiously on Claire's small shoulder blades. She didn't seem to mind; she was too busy peering into the darkness on either side of us.

"Erin!" she called out. "Erin! Where are you!"

I joined in the call, because it was one way of making sure the bears stayed away.

The Small House and the Big House were both lit up now; Stu must have gone into every room and turned on every light. The gravel of the path up from the working beach was soft gray in all the light, and the shape of Stu came lurching down it.

"Hey," he yelled out at us. "Erin?"

If we were Erin, why would we be yelling Erin's name? Stu's face had aged horribly in its concern; the light from the house threw shadow in the divot that ran between his eyes. "Oh," he said. "There you are, Mira. Claire told you? I can't find Erin."

"Where was the last place that you saw her?" I asked, and Stu didn't even flinch at the inanity of the question—Erin was not a set of keys. His eyes were scanning the patch of water that was lit up with the reflection of the Big House lights. Confronted with the water, and the fact that he was looking at the water, seemed to awaken him to the possibility that Erin might be in the water; she might be drowned.

"She was by the Small House. She had come to—she wanted to talk. Have you seen her? Did she say anything? Was she upset?" He laced his fingers.

"I haven't seen her since dinner," I said, and Claire added, "We were doing the dishes."

"Chef," said Stu, turning. "I have to ask Chef." He pointed at me and then Claire. "You," he said to me, "take her back to the Big House. Stay there. Don't go anywhere."

We followed Stu up the path. "We can watch the rest of *Freaky Friday*," I said to Claire, and she said, "I finished it."

Claire's face, once we got inside, was ecstatic. "Where is she! Nobody knows!"

.

During the previous school year, my parents had been under the impression that I was failing all my classes because I was engaged in theft, or hard drugs. Why else would I be flunking out?

"We're nervous for you," they said, and it took all my effort— a great lonely rotating sphere inside of me—to stand at the end of the hall and say, "That's okay."

They didn't believe the truth, probably because it was uninteresting. I was failing because I never showed up. Instead, I'd walk through the quiet subdevelopments, or sit in the molded orange plastic seats outside Sprinkles Donuts, or take a nap on the well-tended lawn of Primrose Creek Park. I would wake up in bewilderment at the bright white sky above me and the plummeting realization that I was, in fact, not waking up the next morning and not one day closer to being back in the Kodiak Archipelago, getting it right this time.

·

Claire fell from high excitement into sleep, curled up in the afghan. I watched a DVD called *Kodiak: Island of the Great Bear*, and also watched the reflection of me and Claire on the couch, both blue-lit from the TV, in the black of the large living room window.

Half an hour later, Erin and Stu walked through the door. Erin's pants were muddy at the knee, and it was clear that they'd both been crying, but she was intact. Stu gave Erin a long hug and then walked silently out. Erin stood by the sink, gulping water.

"Where were you?" I asked.

"I went up the water line, just to think for a second. I guess I didn't notice how late it was. Hi, Claire."

"She's back," Claire said groggily to me. "Nothing happened."

"Nothing happened," said Erin, filling her water glass again.

"It was all a big misunderstanding." The dachshunds had woken up in the commotion and waggled over toward Erin.

"You sure you're okay?" I said. "Everyone was worried."

"I'm sorry you were worried," Erin said, and ruffled Judy's ears. "Who's a Judy, Judy, Judy."

.

When Stu eventually moved in with Erin—they moved to Homer after selling the property on Lavender Island to a couple from Washington State with degrees in ecotourism—he bought her dachshunds. I saw them on his Facebook page, back when he had a Facebook page, before he died.

What I imagine is that Stu had said they were for him when they leaped wriggling out of the car. But I also bet he watched Erin with a tender anticipation of her own tenderness toward the dogs and, by and by, stopped taking care of them altogether. They were hers to feed and wash: she walked to the harbor on bluebird days and in near-gale winds, with the dogs trotting beside her.

This is what I imagine: that only after ten years, when Stu got sick and was bad company, did Erin begin to really appreciate the dachshunds. They were bouncy even in their canine middle age. They couldn't help but wriggle after baths and when they were especially cozy.

I've imagined Stu and Erin's life often; I've imagined Stu's death often. Here's what I think: before his death, he mostly sat near the window and looked out at the water. He assured Erin she was the only woman he had ever really loved and looked on as she stroked the dachshunds' bellies in front of the wood-burning stove like a man looking at, if not his wife and children, then at least his pregnant wife.

I imagine he would have stayed at home until the end, even when his chair was swapped out for a hospital bed. She made him mashed potatoes often. She either slept nearby or, with the help of a baby monitor, slept in their real bed with the dachshunds. One night she heard him cry out, through the monitor, "Is anyone there? Are you there? Are you there?" but she could tell by the gummy quality of his voice that he was sleeping. He needed to rest. "Are you there?" he kept saying. But to wake him up would only confuse him further.

One afternoon, when she was rubbing Eucerin into his dry hands and arms, and into skin that had gotten shiny as he had sickened, as if there was fluid trapped immediately underneath, he smiled at her and said, "Thank you, Maureen." She smiled back and he turned contentedly to watch the fishing boats leaving the harbor. He didn't say the name Maureen again, though—at the end, when he called through the baby monitor with a voice that was suddenly alert and hale, he said, "Hey, Erin!"

This is also what I imagine: when Stu found Erin hiding that night by the water line, when she was crying and getting the seat of her sweatpants all wet by sitting in a patch of grass, he had told her that she was the love of his life. She was crying, not out of any terrible remorse—although that was there and would occasionally sting—but because of the sudden ferocity of her love. The initial ache had been nice, I imagine, that same ache that had been there with her crushes, or when she watched movies starring Daniel Day-Lewis. The rapaciousness was nice, too.

But the new part of it, the living part, the part that felt like the physical memory of the current after spending the day swimming in the river—that part was horrible. It drained the flash and humor out of the world. Suddenly, things were dangerous. There were not only dangerous things that could cause Stu harm and pain, but things that could cause him fear, or sorrow.

.  .  .

After Stu died, Erin left Homer. She went to Hawaii, which she'd come to know as the other state, besides Alaska, that attracted people like her.

So she enrolled in nursing school in Honolulu. It was a big city, true, but nothing dictated that she had to stay there for very long. There were five other islands she could live on. Walking off the plane into the terminal, she felt the air from outside coming through the joints of the gangway. It was a little like the air of Kodiak—the sharpness, not of pine, but of another plant as of yet unidentified. She almost felt eighteen again.

.

In the morning, Chef turned to Claire. "How was the movie?"

"It was great, thanks."

"Not one for movies," he said. That surprised me, because I thought that sadness like Chef's soaked up anything on a screen. And he didn't seem to have hobbies. He didn't seem to enjoy the kinds of things that old men enjoy. He had no interest in the natural world. No bird-watching; no other sports. He wasn't even interested in leering at us.

·

For the rest of her stay, Claire was happy to stay mostly indoors. She spent her time like I did: a long spell in the Bake Shop, a trip down to burn the combustibles, a slow march to the end of the beach to put out the trash. The rest of the time, she read from a book that appeared to be, based on its cover, a story about an insect who was also a detective. In the Bake Shop, I let her eat cookie dough.

"I'll write to you," she said.

But as we were waiting for the seaplane to come pick her up, she didn't repeat the promise. "I have a pottery class next week," she said with the dull affect of someone who doesn't believe on Friday that Monday will ever really show up. "At the Coast Guard base. Me and Chrissie will take it together."

"Who's Chrissie?" I asked.

"Oh, Chrissie," she said, waving her hand in the way, I suspected, that Chrissie waved hers. I had never seen Claire do anything like that. "She's my best friend in the whole world."

CHAPTER 8

Claire left in the morning; Maureen and Polly wouldn't be back until mid-evening. I spent most of the day in my newly empty bedroom, masturbating intently. No matter how much I tried to integrate what I knew of Alaskan fashion, Ed kept wearing incongruous leather driving gloves. His eyes: filled with fury or pain.

"Are you okay?" I'd ask.

"I'm not okay," he'd say. "And it's your fault."

"I didn't do anything."

His face, weighted with lust, would elongate. "You're going to," he'd say, and stuff one of his gloved fingers into my mouth.


Later, shuffling from the Bake Shop door, I saw Erin and Stu standing in the Greenhouse. She was tending some chives and he stood behind her, head bent and smelling the place where her sweatshirt hood draped away from the nape of her neck. I kicked a patch of gravel, and Erin folded herself over the chives, now absorbed in patting the potting soil. Stu turned his crouch over Erin's neck into a reach for the shears and then came out of the Greenhouse, jauntily patting his open palm with the shears blades.

"Ahoy, Baker!" he said. "And what are you baking up today?"

"Snickerdoodles," I said, and he laughed one of his big booming dining room laughs.

"Snickerdoodles—what a wonderful name," he said. He stopped and flared his nostrils. "It always smells so good next to the Bake Shop."

•

The Vermonters arrived in a Sammy's Air seaplane. They were a family made tidy by a certain amount of wealth and even more outdoorsiness: the mother and the daughter could slot their ponytails through the hole at the back of their matching baseball caps in one fluid motion.

I was already making my way up the beach when I heard Stu calling, "The bounty of Alaska! Salmon from the sea! Berries from the bushes! Beer from the creeks!" Maureen's laughter was rat-a-tatting above the trees. The Vermonters were going to stay in Guest Cabin 3, the one with the best view. I'd placed a bouquet of fireweed in their bathroom.

When I returned to the beach for the parents' suitcases, I saw that things had advanced in an orderly manner. Maureen was standing near the mother and daughter, Erin flanked her, and Polly flanked her in turn. Stu was over at the fish table, gutting a red salmon. The Vermonter boy moaned delightedly at the sight.

·

"Jellies," Stu's voice squawked over the VHF radio the next morning, and Maureen said, "Dear Lord. Mira! Where is the condensed milk?"

The fishing party had turned around: the silver skiff was motoring on the silver water at high speed toward land. I was standing in the kitchen, my midsection damp from sloshed sink water and my shirt clinging to my belly. Maureen crouched down, looking through the lower cabinets. The outboard motor on the skiff shut off, and through the open kitchen windows we heard the agitated scrabble of shale chips.

"Evaporated milk!" Maureen said, wheeling her hand to indicate speed and urgency. "Mira! Look alive! We have jellyfish stings to take care of!"

The evaporated milk was in the Bake Shop, a whole drawer of it. I had never used evaporated milk for anything. As a child, I'd picked it out for donation at canned food drives because I liked the idea of poor people spooning it delightedly into their mouths and beaming at the fat content. I think I had seen that in a movie about the Blitz, except maybe the people were eating rationed jam. In any case, the entire idea of evaporated milk seemed antique.

By the time I had come back from the Bake Shop, a can of Carnation in each hand, Maureen was gone. The kitchen door was open, and I could see that all the kitchen cabinets had been flung open, too. The last diminishing crunches could be heard from the beach; Maureen had finished running down. I jogged after, pumping the cans of Carnation like hand weights.

The men—Stu, the Vermonter husband, and the Vermonter son—were standing to the side, looking helpless, and Maureen was down on her knees, attending to the Vermonter wife's face. The little Vermonter girl was still sitting in the skiff, which had been half pulled up on the beach. Her little blond head was dwarfed by her life jacket. No one was crying, but the Vermonter wife's breathing was ragged—relief after pain. When she turned her head, I could see that her face was strung with ribbons of evaporated milk.

"There, now," said Maureen. Maureen set down the can of Carnation, took a packet of wet wipes from her fleece vest, and cleaned the Vermonter wife's face tenderly. "Evaporated milk takes care of the jelly stings. All better?"

"All better. It wasn't that bad."

"It wasn't that bad at all, was it? But you want to attend to a jelly sting as soon as possible; the little nematocysts can burrow." Maureen turned to me but was asking the Vermonters: "Want some tea? Coffee?" I readied myself to sprint back up the hill.

But the Vermonters, the man consoling his son and the woman her daughter, wanted to go back out.

"It's jelly weather," Maureen said. "You can almost see the bloom from here." There were a few moon jellies caught up among the rocks at the tide line, pale deflated sacks.

"We saw them swimming," said the boy. "They look like ghosts!"

"They don't swim," said the Vermonter husband. "They float." There was a dimpling on the water a hundred yards out that could have been a jelly bloom touching the surface, or a little rivulet caused by the wind.

"What people tell you is that you're supposed to pee on a jelly sting," said Stu. "But that's just for tourists. You're *guests*."

"Eww," screamed the children.

"Evaporated milk is the thing for jelly stings," said Stu.

"Stu. I just said that," said Maureen.

•

Maureen had assigned Erin and Polly chores around the homestead. Erin had slept late. As Maureen and I came back into the Big House, we saw Erin moving toward the stairs with a mug of coffee, using the tiny, shuffling steps you need when you're wearing thick socks on hardwood. Polly was in the sunroom, sitting cross-legged like a child on a mat and stroking the sleepy dachshunds.

I sidled my wet midsection up to the sink again. Maureen stood next to me, resting her fingertips gently at the lip of the counter. She lifted them up and placed them down again, lining up her nail beds with the counter's edge, or following some other sort of soothing geometry. It was an attempt at comfort, but it failed, and she took a mug from the cupboard and filled it with coffee and then added more milk and sugar than I had ever seen her take. She looked up, she looked at the floor, nodding slightly, like she was counting in her head.

"It's jelly weather. Maybe a jelly week," she said. "There was an extra can of evaporated milk in the pantry."


I've been there, now, that place of gray internal weather where the jellyfish bloom keeps rising and rising. I know now the need for adding extra cream and sugar to your coffee, or touching a countertop in order to convince yourself that you have fingers and can touch countertops, or counting or saying the ABCs or repeating a phrase—any phrase, but the phrase I've found myself chanting in moments of absolute panic is "soft sweater," because it's the most comforting thing I can think of, so I keep saying it in my head over and over—breathe in and allow yourself all the panic you want, but on the breath out you need to say only "soft sweater, soft sweater, soft sweater," and imagine touching a very fine angora sweater. But when I saw Maureen that day, feebly touching the countertop and lifting the mug of coffee to her lips and smacking them in dainty horror at the amount of sugar she'd allowed herself to put in, I just thought she was pathetic and old and horrible.

Maureen walked off with her mug. I scrubbed a sausage gravy pot with a handled brush. Above us, the beams squeaked—Erin was walking across the floor, getting dressed. From the sun-room came the sounds of Polly saying, "Who's a Ruby, Ruby, Ruby, Ruby, Ruby?"

.

Polly loved animals, which is something I didn't understand until I became friends with a woman who loved, above all things, her dog. She said to me, "I could never date a man who didn't love animals." I think this meant she was looking for someone with the ability to love without keeping a tally system of faults and grievances and items owed and affection earned. I can't be sure; her dog bit me.

I don't love animals in the way that animals are supposed to be loved, because I keep thinking of them as people trapped in animal bodies. When I interact with an animal, I try to extrapolate its behavior after assigning it a human personality—Ruby was an aging diva, Judy was a manservant—and then, when they fail to live up to my expectations, I'll feel regretful but not intrigued. Instead of thinking, "What vast tundra is the human personality," and feeling as though the world was opening up for me, unfolding until, like on the tundra, it is impossible to differentiate the houses from the clouds and mountains from puddles of water, I'll just think, "I got that wrong, then. Ruby is not an aging diva."

Polly didn't take her gap year in Southeast Asia that year. From what I pieced together, she went home and worked in an animal shelter, first as a volunteer and then as an outreach coordinator. Then she went to college on her field-hockey scholarship. Her first picture on Facebook was of her with a collegiate sweatshirt, holding a hockey stick.

Then the pictures changed. It seems that she preferred to take runs alone or with a group of girls from Track and Field. They were long-legged, lean girls who already showed the beginnings of smile lines and liked camping. I imagine that Polly would have been cowed by them at first, partially because they exhibited an echo of the physical bravado of Erin. She'd have felt round and comical beside them. But I believe they took her in; they were all women who understood the lonely happiness of running, which could then make way for the happy camaraderie of sitting around a fire, twisting potatoes into tinfoil, and telling ghost stories.

After college, Polly went on an extended trip through Southeast Asia. She saw Angkor Wat at dawn and stayed for a week at a Buddhist convent. I imagine her moving about the grounds, not speaking.

She'd been given the task of sweeping the paths that led into the jungle. It was a tedious job—the leaves simply had to be swept to the side. It was perhaps another exercise in meditation, she couldn't be sure, but it reminded her of checking the water line at Lavender Island, and she laid her broom down and cried until another woman came over and silently hugged her. The other time she cried during that trip was when she drank too much at a party in Mui Ne and waded out into the water and vomited. Otherwise, she smiled at everything and returned home suntanned and exhausted from too little structure to her days. Then she adopted her first dog, a young mutt with a torn ear.

·

"And here we have Alaskan wild-nettle sauté with shallots."

"Before the lodge, we were setnetters," Maureen told the Vermonters. "Right at the point."

She traced the curl of the point on the dining room table. The Vermonters craned their necks, looking out the window. You couldn't see the point out the dining room window; you could only see the point from the living room window and the sunroom. That's where Polly and Erin were sitting, eating silently. I had gone in there with the bowl of wild-nettle sauté. Erin had smiled dazedly up at me; Polly was looking at her plate, mashing her potatoes with her fork tines.

"Where's the point?" asked the Vermonter husband.

"Right at the tip of the point," Maureen said again, retracing on the dining room table.

"It's right thataway," said Stu, pointing into the dining room wall. "More wine?"

"Oh," said the Vermonter husband. "Why not?"

"It's hard work," Maureen said. "You're crawling along the net in the skiff, and just picking the fish, picking the salmon out of the net. You end up ankle deep, calf deep in salmon."

"Calf deep in money!" said Stu, and laughed toward the Vermonters. The Vermonter woman put her fork down; we were eating Baked Alaskan Red Salmon.

"Or moon jellies," said Maureen. "There was a week of jelly weather at the beginning—Stu, remember? And then there's no fish in the net; instead, you have a net that's clotted with moon jellies. It's really—it's like Knox gelatin. And they *smell* when there are so many of them. They have this distinct smell—a bit like dish detergent."

"Eww," said the Vermonter children, and they started laughing. I was standing in the doorway with more potatoes, but Stu gave me a look that made me back up and place the potatoes on a trivet near the stove. There was a pause while the Vermonters waited for Maureen to continue. But she was staring at the point she had traced on the tabletop.

"Jellies aside, I'm glad we got to spend the day fishing together," said Stu. "But you'll get more of me on the Susitna Spirit. I'm flying into town right after dinner, but I'll be coming back out in a couple of days, and then it's on to Katmai."

Maureen looked up. "We'll have a grand old time together right here!" she said. "Tomorrow we can take out the kayaks. It's really magical to be that close to the water. Erin and Polly will join us; they're great guides."

"Polly will join you," said Stu. "I'll need Erin with me on the Susitna Spirit. She's like the first mate."

"You won't need her this time, surely," said Maureen, smiling. "You're just picking up the next guests and coming back out."

"I will, yes," said Stu. "It's always nice to have someone else on board when we navigate Marmot Pass." Marmot Pass was a cute name but a dreadful location in the archipelago: swarms of water that curled into eddies over unseen rocks, and a terrible tidal pull.

"Oh, Stu!" said Maureen. "He's too modest. Back when we were homesteaders, he could navigate Marmot Pass with one hand tied behind his back. Erin should stay here."

"Right, right, right," said Stu. "We'll discuss this later. Who wants more wine?" He filled his glass.

"Or potatoes?" I said from the doorway.

"This wild-nettle sauté is amazing," said Maureen. "Chef, well done!" Chef was already back in his tent cabin.

·

Stu and Maureen stayed back in the dining room while Polly and Erin brought the Vermonters down to the firepit.

"She's invaluable," I heard Stu say. "We'll sleep on board the Susitna Spirit and come out here first thing in the morning."

"Two seaplane tickets in the high season? Are you out of your mind?" said Maureen.

"Okay," said Stu. He was dangerously amicable. "Then here's what I'll do: I'll go to Kodiak alone. I'll pick up the Karlsson group in the morning, and then I'll get them out here and drop them off. I'll do all that alone. Then I'll pick up the Bascoms, but I'll also pick up Erin, if you don't mind, because I can't do the Katmai trip on the Susitna Spirit all by myself."

"Stu," said Maureen, and it was both a plea and a warning.

•

Later, on my way to take the trash to the tide line, I saw Erin and Stu sitting at the firepit. Stu was laughing, and, rather than the hearty donkey laugh of dinnertime and guests, it was a hiccupping giggle. Oh, I thought, he's been pretending to be happy this whole time.

•

When I came back, there was a commotion by the mudroom. Stu and Erin were cleaning their shoes.

"I bet it was that little brat," said Stu, gesturing toward Guest Cabin 3 with his thumb.

"What happened?" I asked Polly. Her eyes got very wide.

"I guess some fish guts got into Stu's and Erin's shoes," she said. "Somehow!"

•

Late that night, after Stu had flown out to pick up the next guests in Kodiak, the weather turned.

The rocker in the living room of the Big House swayed in a storm, a small squeak, impossible to hear over the clinking of the sea-glass nodes of the mobile. It swayed like a ship, especially in a williwaw down from the mountains. It swayed like a cradle.

The house settled at night: one long creak from one side one night, one long creak from the other side the next. It creaked into our beds and into our dreams; it lulled and agitated us in equal measure. I don't know if the Small House creaked; it looked very solid there, up on the hill, on the overlook. It probably didn't creak in Chef's tent cabin; the floorboards were settled into the joists, which were settled into the earth that was always wet or always frozen.

The dachshunds didn't squeak in a storm; they lay there, snout to tail, curled, with fur moving upward and down as the light moved upward and down along their backs. The Greenhouse didn't move, but the small shoots of the herbs in their orderly beds shuddered. A watering can fell off a plywood shelf, but that could have been because it was put back absentmindedly. No one ran through the storm: there was no need to run, because it was cozy and dry inside your rain gear. I wore it—rain gear over fleece vest over sweatshirt over turtleneck, and extra socks inside Xtratufs. I wore a Twins baseball cap, and the hood of my sweatshirt up over that, and the orange hood of the rain gear over that. The baseball cap was necessary so the rain-gear hood didn't flop into your eyes.

The day of the big storm—the wind flattening the alders so that all you saw was the silver side of their leaves, seagulls blowing haplessly across the water like scraps of tissue—the Vermonters were forced to stay inside. The water was all whitecaps, and there could be no kayaking. Their trip to Katmai, scheduled for that evening, would be delayed. Hiking was possible, if they wanted to do that. Alaskans didn't let weather get between them and doing what they wanted to do, unless it was truly dangerous out on the water. Did they want to hike? Otherwise, Maureen said, maybe the best thing was a quiet one. Potentially, the weather would clear up in the late afternoon, and everyone could take a sunset kayak.

The Vermonters paid attention to the wishes of their children. The walk down from the cabins to the Big House had left the fleece of their jackets matted; the tip of the Vermonter girl's ponytail dripped onto the buffed hardwood floor. The girl wanted to read; the boy was stretching into the last growth spurt before adolescence, and he wanted to go back to sleep.

"A little extra sleep never hurt anyone," said Maureen, and she instructed the Vermonters to take off their wet fleeces. She handed them to me; I would put them in the dryer, and they'd be toasty warm as soon as the Vermonters had finished breakfast. Then I could slip into some rain gear, get four sets of rain gear from the gear shed, and bring them back for the Vermonters to use as they walked back to their cabin. It was called rain gear for a reason!

·

In Hanoi, I was friends with a man named Deniz. He'd been addicted to morphine, a fact that left me cold. Morphine wasn't very sleazy. But Deniz had lived in New Mexico, and he wore the mantle of New Mexico in the way that I wore the mantle of Alaska; it defined and vivified him.

New Mexico was terribly high up, more than a mile in altitude. It was on top of a steep plateau. In Albuquerque, I had heard, all roads look as if they're going downhill. I could feel the unease, something like my neck craning back too far, thinking about life at a mile up.

And was morphine like that? I asked him. Something of that steepness, some kind of ascent? It was the beginning of the night in early autumn, the ringing sound of people selling street food echoing off the courtyard walls. We were only twenty-three: there was time for everything. Deniz had gotten off morphine, and he wasn't yet backsliding, buying effervescent codeine tablets in bulk. No, said Deniz, looking like he was talking about an infant daughter, no, it was nothing like that. What morphine was like was this: it was like having a snow day in middle school, and your mom comes in early because she's seen the weather report, and she pats your head and says, low, that there's no school on account of the snow but she still has to go into work. And she leaves her hand on your head a little, and tucks the side of the duvet in around you, and you're relieved, because you're growing so hard you frequently feel a deep skeletal ache and you're desperately tired. And you snuggle your face into your pillow and inhale, exhale, until you're breathing at the cadence of a sleeping person even though you're not quite asleep, so you hold off sleep just a little, a small erotic game, because the sleep is creeping up your legs and you know you'll sleep until eleven or noon, until you're satiated and the skeletal muscles have repaired themselves, and when you wake up you won't ache, and then—*then* there's the memory of a trip recently made to the grocery store, there are pudding cups in the refrigerator, and a whole bag of Bugles, and you'll have whatever you'd like and *then,* then there's unsupervised internet access, which means all the porn you'd like, not having to cram it in but really savoring it all, work doesn't end until five p.m. And then there's TV to watch. All of that is ahead of you, plus time to sleep. That's what morphine is like.

•

That's what morphine is like: a snow day or a storm day. The Vermonters are welcome to come into the Big House and watch a DVD; dinner will be at the usual time. At lunch, Mira will bring you a basket with sandwiches and chips and apples and cookies—use the s'mores basket, put a different napkin in it, maybe one of the good striped dish towels, cover it all with plastic wrap against the rain. The cookies will be fresh baked; the morning will be spent in the Bake Shop. The heat from the big black oven will shimmer in front of rain-striped windows.

When the Vermonter mother opens the Guest Cabin door, she'll reveal a family in matching flannel pajama sets: Black Watch plaid for the girls, MacTavish for the boys. The nice dusty smell of the electric heater. She'll take the basket with a smile; the children are absorbed with a portable DVD player, and there's no need to go to the Big House. The Vermonter mother will scan from the porch, past the water streaming down the drainpipe to the smoke from the woodstove in the Big House being flown across its eaves like a seagull, the light getting deeper blue above the rills and rills of whitecaps out on the water.

They have all afternoon; she can lie in the double bed, in the crook of her husband's arm, as he finishes a John le Carré novel; the kids can take another DVD from the accordion folder. They can eat more chips—Maureen insisted that a whole bag be packed instead of just handfuls in individual sandwich bags, because these guests are missing out on an Alaskan day, one rare day when the weather proves too much for the clothing.

But this is important for the Vermonter mother, this day—she can play house, still slipping into girlhood after all these years, playing that this is her homestead, her island; the weather is proving a respite from *her* work, and as she falls asleep, to the chatter of the Disney movie and her husband flipping the page, she'll fall into an old reverie where there is no husband and no children and somehow she's still looking up to the Disney princesses, who are sixteen or fourteen. Somehow, in falling asleep on the rare bad weather day, the taste of sour cream and onion chips in her mouth, she's seven or eight again.

Chef was in his tent cabin. The weather must have been billowing the walls. Maureen, regal, was composed on the Big House sofa, Ruby or Judy in the crook of her lap. Erin was sleeping on her back, mouth open, on her bed. Polly was curled into a snail, tucked under an afghan, on the recliner. Her eyes were wide, and she was still except for her feet, which paddled back and forth within the afghan.

I took the tide booklet out of the central pocket of my hoodie and ran my golf pencil until I found the date. Low tide was now: time to get back into my rain gear and take the trash out. Tomorrow was forecasted to be a bluebird day.

•

The next morning, the Vermonters packed up their neat luggage, and we hauled it to the beach. Stu arrived, sleep-deprived but so flushed with love he looked younger than he had ever looked—his eyes were twenty. He had picked up the new guests—Swedes—brought them easily through Marmot Pass in the Susitna Spirit, and brought them to shore in the skiff. Now he was dropping off the Swedes and picking up the Vermonters and Erin to take them bear watching on the Katmai Peninsula.

Lavender Island, at the twilight side of the bay and dim every evening, was basking in the full morning light. There was already a slant to it, and the beach smelled autumnal, something of the charcoal sweetness of the inside of a jack-o'-lantern, because of the debris brought down from the williwaw—great brambles, snarls of alder leaves, and some crispy heather that must have been scaled off the very top of the mountain, all tangled up behind the logs that delineated the tide line.

There were the Vermonters, fed full of oatmeal, waiting for Katmai. There were the Swedes—Arvid & Co.!—hopping off the Susitna Spirit. They were almost as tall as the Norwegians, and several of them were gingers.

"Are you brothers?" said Maureen in merry surprise. And they said, "Cousins." Maureen had been joking, or trying to joke, standing next to Stu, beaming with his twenty-year-old eyes, and Erin, sparkling down the entire beach with her duffel bag. Erin, locking arms with the Vermonter mother and telling her, "The bear watching in Katmai is amazing," but shining everything in the direction of Stu, who held his face up to the thin sunshine and said, in the direction of the Vermonter husband, "We have great weather for the passage; you might even be able to see Fourpeaked Glacier—what a treat."

Stu swung his gaze over Erin's head, a passing over that was as tender as kissing her temple. He addressed the Vermonter mother, saying, "Erin and I are going to take your bags up into the Susitna Spirit right quick; hold tight." And then they were trailing away on the skiff, leaving long scratches in the otherwise flat water, not speaking—sound carries over water—just alert and standing far apart. When the motor stopped next to the Susitna Spirit Maureen's face was fixed in a smile. It was clear that bringing the bags belowdecks was an excuse for a kiss—probably only a kiss because they both had rain gear on and who would want to fumble through rain gear that was always, inevitably, shedding little rainbow fish scales that had stuck there wet and then dried but maybe they were also fucking, terribly quickly and terribly urgently.

Maureen nodded to Polly, who was looking drowned. Maureen also looked drowned; with her dandelion-down hair pulling away from her ponytail, she looked as if she were being buoyed in all directions by water. Polly grabbed two Swedish duffel bags, and I grabbed the other two, and we headed toward the cabins, listening to Maureen say, "The nice thing about Alaska is that we don't let a little weather come between us and doing what we want to do," even though we had just let the williwaw get between the Vermonters and their kayaking adventure, and even though, like the Norwegians before them, the Swedes understood intimately the nature of life at the top of the globe. From beneath the alders, as the shale path gave way to gravel, I heard, "You're not from Stockholm; where are you from?" and the Swedes said, "Yes. We are from Stockholm."

When we came back down to the beach, the skiff full of Vermonters was nearly back at the Susitna Spirit. Maureen was still speaking to the Swedes, who were confused.

"We did have breakfast on the boat," said one, as Maureen

was saying, "We have a lot of piping hot oatmeal." Maureen shuffled her hands. "Ah," she said. "That's Alaskan hospitality. We always overfeed you!"

"It's true that Americans are very fat people," said a Swede. I held my hands protectively over my black-and-white-striped midsection.

Maureen laughed, looking out at the Susitna Spirit. Her hair floated. The rattle of the anchor being pulled was somehow clearer in the coppery light. A boom of Stu's laughter cracked across the water. "Yes," she said absently, "it's important to keep a healthy lifestyle."

The Swedes were to have a few days of fly-fishing, kayaking, and hiking while the Vermonters were on the Susitna Spirit in Katmai. Then Sammy of Sammy's Air would pick up the Vermonters from Katmai, Erin and Stu would cross the Shelikof, pick up the Swedes, and go right back out. The Swedes would round out their week as the Vermonters had done before them: with bear viewing, fishing, and lazy crawls along the National Park coastline.

The first day, while Chef hid in his tent cabin and Polly and

Maureen packed the Swedes into kayaks, I sat on the counter of the Bake Shop, waiting for the ding of the egg timer.

I stared dead-eyed, trying to project, again and again, the moment from the first time Ed and I would meet onto that blank white wall. I would see him on the street. I would be walking, and he would be walking toward me. No; he'd turn a corner and we'd bump. No; we'd be walking toward each other, for maybe half a block. We'd stare at each other for the entirety of the walk. No; I wouldn't notice him until he was right in front of me, and I'd look up and say, "Hello, Ed." We'd kiss frantically—no; I wanted to take my time.

Then we'd walk back to his apartment—no. (What would we do on the walk?)

We'd arrange to get a coffee and sit, staring. He'd touch my hand, and it would feel—but we'd still have to walk back to his place.

I would be in his apartment already, somehow. I would be in a dress (unlikely in Kodiak in November; not impossible). I would be reading on his couch, with my feet up on his coffee table.

And what then? He'd come in; I'd stand. "Hello, Ed."

I was straining a bit. I was worried that my memory of Ed's eyes had become the memory of my memory of his eyes.

When he was at my aunt's cabin, Ed had listened to a burned CD. There was one lolloping reggae song he'd sing, under his breath, rolling cigarettes. After he left, I listened to that song; after I left, I found the track, bought the CD, listened to the song in my room with the door locked, lying on top of my comforter, too paralyzed by the dance of the images of the previous summer to move. But, as it turned out, I could only listen to the song so many times.

The egg timer dinged. I took the snickerdoodles from their tray, shook them neatly onto cooling racks. I set the egg timer. It was almost time for Maureen and Polly and the Swedes to come back from kayaking, which meant I'd have to scrub the cookie trays on the double and get down to the beach to help put the kayaks up. Then—I'd checked the tide booklet—it was time to take the trash down to below the tide line.

•

Polly asked if I wanted to go on a hike; magnanimously, I said yes. We walked the entirety of the working beach, right up until the crescent petered out, and then climbed up the rocks and into the forest. The forest floor was springy, and we both affected the air of being younger than we were, bouncing from mossy stone to mossy log, and cracking thin branches off mossy trees.

"I know it was stupid to put the fish guts in their shoes," said Polly. "But it was satisfying." She began breaking her stick into smaller and smaller pieces, staring intently into the crosshatch of the tree branches.

"Did you know that Stu kissed me?" she said. "Last summer? He did. At the water line. He kissed me. And then he told me that he wanted me to come back this summer." And I wish she had cried, so I could do something, but all she did was keep snapping at the bundle of twigs in her hand. Then the moment for consolation was over.

"Nobody knows," said Polly. "Don't tell Maureen. Definitely don't tell Erin." I bobbed my head at her, because her eyes were searching the branches and my face for something to reassure her.

"I won't," I said. "I won't. But why are you staying here?"

"I can't go home yet," she said. "Do you know how much it costs to go to Southeast Asia?"

I didn't, but I knew how much it cost to rent a room in Kodiak. I knew exactly how far five thousand dollars would go.

.

Polly had made me feel claustrophobic; her fantasies probably had more heft than mine. She had more memories; they
were vivid. The previous year, that kiss near the top of the
mountain—*that* was something. You could build a solid, beautiful future around a memory like that.

Here's what I imagined: Polly hadn't been held against a chest
that thick. His beard stubble too long to rasp, the little provocation of his tongue, and a little terror—she couldn't decide what
to focus on because there was too much: the smell of the pushki,
the shade of the sky, the pressure of his chest, or the way both
thumbs—he held her face in his hands—kept stroking with
reassurance at the sides of her cheeks.

And then, afterward, the looks. She'd been anxious for them,
dodging about the dining room, skipping, sparkly. And when
they were alone, there they were, those shimmering moments
that would stain the backs of her eyelids; she sat on one couch
and he sat on the other, close enough to touch. His legs were
spread wide, the ball of each hand on each knee. Both of them
speaking with their chins down and their eyes up, so that their

eyes, their looking, was the only thing on their face. That would stay with her. She'd look at the light on in the Small House and her chest would flip. When he came in from a shower, the only thing she could think was "He's been naked recently."

There were four beds total in the Big House. There was a double bed in the Small House, Guest Cabins filled with beds. In the sunroom, there was the dog bed shared by Ruby and Judy. On fine days, there was the possibility of soft moss up the water line. In the gear sheds, piles of soft fishing nets to lie on.

Then watching the shape of him retreat up the path from the working beach as she took the tender back to Kodiak at the end of the summer. During the school year, she'd look at the pictures she'd taken, again and again. She'd look at his face in photographs until he seemed ready to speak to her. She watched movies about young women and older men, and each of them shocked her with desire and with the portents they held for her own life.

When those images faded, when the memory of his thumbs on her cheeks became instead the memory of her holding her own face like he had held it, backward, her own hands too soft, she grew angry. Those memories had been hers by rights, and she had tarnished them. They had been her toys, and she had worn them out by playing with them too often. She could only blame herself.

So, instead, she reached forward into her future, where the fantasies were played in the past tense, just like memories. Maureen slid gracefully away—she gave Maureen a lover, some old dapper gentleman, maybe Italian. In fact, it was Maureen who had decided to leave Stu, for a strapping widower. They sailed off. Then it was just Polly and Stu on the island.

Or—a storm. Maureen dies without much pain. Polly saves Stu, holds his head in her hands. "You've saved me." He regains his strength instantly.

Or—a bear. That was a good threat, and the main danger apart from the elements. Maureen gets (stupidly) between a mother bear and her cubs and is torn to shreds. No one sees this, because that would be too grisly. They find her fleece vest on the beach near the tide line. Stu is distraught, violently distraught, and pushes Polly against a beam in the Small House and rips her clothes like a bear.

All these fantasies were suspended above Polly's head, these multicolored stories with their dazzling twists and their predictable endings, throughout the entire year. Polly studied these futures, she added to them as she fell asleep. When she emailed with Maureen in the early spring, she was asked, "Would you like to bring a friend along? We could use the extra pair of hands."

.

"How do you say 'cheers' in Swedish?" asked Maureen. "I try to learn how to say 'cheers' in every language."

"It's 'skål,' " said one of the ginger Swedes.

"Ah!" said Maureen, heartily. She hoisted her glass of wine. "Skål!"

"How do you say 'cheers' in Chinese?" said another Swede.

"In Chinese?" asked Maureen.

"Yes. I have a business trip there this autumn."

"I don't know," said Maureen.

"I thought you learned 'cheers' in every language?"

"I try," said Maureen. "But I don't know every one."

"Mandarin is an important language," he said, and his cousin said, "You know it, Arvid: it's 'gānbēi.' Similar to 'kanpai.' "

"Well, it all means the same thing, doesn't it!" Maureen laughed with her head back. "Would you like more wine?"

Polly and I were both sitting at the table. Chef had been invited to join, but he wanted to call it an early night. It was my job, Maureen said, to make sure and see that everything was plated nicely, to make sure all the serving utensils were polished, because the guests would be serving themselves. Arvid took the bottle of wine and filled up his glass, and then filled up Maureen's. He filled up Polly's small water glass, which was empty, with wine.

"Why not?" said Maureen, and she threw back her head. "I won't tell if you don't."

"Of course," said one of the ginger Swedes. "She can't drink yet. It's against the American law."

.

The Swedes were in the hot tub; I was scraping the last of the fish into the trash. Maureen and Polly were in the living room.

"I was being polite," said Polly.

"There's polite and there's polite," said Maureen. "You can politely decline. You can say no, and still be polite. It's polite to do the right thing and say no. I could get in trouble—did you think of that?"

"We had beer on the Fourth of July," said Polly, very small. "Stu said we could."

" 'Stu said.' Stu isn't here. You could have said no. The wine is for guests. For guests. Wine costs money. And it's illegal. Did you think of that? If anyone found out, I could get in trouble. Did you think of that? That it's illegal?"

"Who? There's no one around to find out," said Polly.

.

After Erin and Stu returned to pick up the Swedes, and after they streamed away again, Maureen threw herself into a frenzy of efficiency. She drowned herself in work. Chef wasn't given anything else to do: he still had to make two meals a day, as usual, but they were smaller and more piecemeal.

I was instructed to expand my horizons in the Bake Shop— maybe we should try biscotti? I was also given the task of deep-cleaning the Big House. I scrubbed the walls; I went over the blond carpets upstairs with a can of carpet cleaner. I polished all the wood surfaces. Between my morning and afternoon chores, I napped violently, and woke up sweating to the buzz and bump of Arctic flies trying to escape through closed windows.

Maureen was exerting herself above and beyond. During the week when Erin and Stu were on the Susitna Spirit, Maureen pulled every spruce needle from between the cracks of the deck, because when spruce needles rotted they caused rot in whatever surrounded them. She re-stained Guest Cabin 2, because when damp got into the wood it was almost as bad as spruce needles. She organized the souvenir shelf in the sunroom. The Lavender Island mugs were emptied of dead bees.

She weed-whacked what had already been weed-whacked—the trails, the edge of the lawn. The hedges were pruned and geometric. The lawn became the lawn of a country manor. She chopped wood; the woodpile grew under its blue tarp. Descending the staircase after my nap, I saw her out on the lawn, on her hands and knees, prying up the clusters of native grasses whose flat leaves stamped the lawn. Later, on my way to the Bake Shop, I saw her doing the same thing to the path that led to the eagles' nest. For a week afterward, until a soft storm rolled in and new grasses sprouted, the path was spotless.

Polly had less to do. There was no one to teach fly-fishing to. Sometimes she helped out with Maureen's chores, but Maureen was doggedly working herself into a state of exhaustion. She let

Polly take over Erin's chores: she was allowed to mow the lawn and tend to the herbs in the Greenhouse, and she was allowed to check the water line.

In the mornings, after we'd had our eggs and coffee, Polly would stuff her pants into her Xtratufs and start the hike up past the Guest Cabins to the water line. In this way, her day started out with purpose; her black curls bounced with intent. She marched up the mountain with a backpack full of electrical tape for leaks and thick gloves for clearing small blockages, but what if something was amiss? A felled tree? A section of pipe broken clean in two? A fawn with a broken leg?

But it was a sound water line, and, although Polly searched the length of the pipe for cracks and pressed her ear to listen for blockages, there was nothing wrong at all. She returned off the mountain with her face lax. There wasn't much else for her to do. She put together two jigsaw puzzles that week. A number of the doorknobs throughout the camp were found to be decorated with damp plugs of chewing gum; I think Polly did that as well.

She followed Maureen around. There was something newly childlike about her, about the way she walked behind Maureen, and how she sat beside Maureen on the couch in the evenings, Maureen looking out the window and Polly leafing through a coffee-table book filled with illustrated plates detailing the natural history of Alaska. You almost expected Polly's legs to be swinging, she looked that small.

·

I imagine Polly ended up just fine. She moved to Oregon—which was less remote but no less outdoorsy than Alaska—where she married a man with a kind expression and a full beard. They lived in the country and kept animals. There was a flurry of domestic drama whenever one of the llamas wandered into the woods.

Like a lot of girls I knew who had approached disintegration— meth, becoming a sugar baby, a mental breakdown—she turned toward the gentle light of the natural. Polly believed in clean living. She had a great deal of affection for the sweet potato. She was quiet and resolute.

When she felt ill-at-ease, Polly took long runs through nature, camping trips, and hikes. When she started to age, she used an oil infused with goji berries on her skin: the bottle deliciously instructed the user to massage the oil and create "an emulsion." She never became superstitious or occult, but she doted on ritual. She took frequent saunas. She drank complex herbal teas that promised renewal.

And it worked. Her skin looked illuminated from within. After she ran or hiked, her eyes were bright, and at the end of the day, she was suffused with a weariness that made her feel cozy. The llamas and her herb garden flourished, and she felt content. There were nights in the winter when she'd startle awake and look up at the immobile ceiling fan, sometimes for hours, but in the morning, over oatmeal, she felt anew the calling of her virtuousness.

She intentionally stayed away from long-term relationships until she was in her late twenties; she was reluctant to stay with anyone who might be primarily interested in her youth. And when she met the man who would become her husband, she checked into his proclivities—was he attracted by the innocent, or schoolgirls, or stepfather-stepdaughter stuff? He wasn't, she realized. When they watched porn together, he seemed to like, more than anything else, large breasts.

She became capable; she built the sauna on their property. She knew what to do with chicken wire. What she did was never done quickly—she had learned that her grace was not in sudden movement. The animals, especially, responded to the fact that she was unhurried. It was a gift. This fact about herself—her agile slowness—had first become apparent to Polly when she saw Erin working at Lavender Island.

CHAPTER 9

It was surprising to hear the screaming coming from the Small House and not see a light on: in my understanding of the universe, screaming necessitated the lighting of lamps. But Maureen and Stu had seen each other so often. Maybe she didn't want to look at him any longer.

There was a late summer heat wave, the last of its kind; the fireweed was turning to pollen on its stems, and the tops of the mountains were crowned with changing heather. The rust was starting at the top of the mountains and making its way down. The noise carried through the open window. I was loading the dishwasher. Chef was nowhere. Polly sat with a dog on her lap. Erin, I found out later, was lying on her bed with a pillow over her head.

The screaming stopped, and then started again. For a good while—the time it took to load all the glasses, at least—the screaming continued. Then, starting in on the hand-wash, there was a period when Stu was speaking too softly to be heard and Maureen's screams would break in. The melody of the screaming was all the same—three staccato beats, rising tone, with the last word being elongated a beat each time. There was a long "i" in that word: I think Maureen was saying, "She's a child," but I can't be sure.

I liked drying the wineglasses with their special soft cloth; that made me feel like a real professional. I held them to the light, watched the mountains widen through them. On the recliner, Polly was lifting the dachshund's ears and letting them fall. I hung the special soft cloth on its special soft cloth hook. I slotted the wineglasses into their rack. There was no noise except a few gulls, and then, also sounding like a gull's meow, the words *No, no, no,* or *go, go, go,* carried out from the Small House.

The floorboards in the upstairs of the Big House squeaked, tracking the location of anyone upstairs. I was always aware of this when I walked to Maureen's desk to get the phone book to look up Ed's name and address, and then to the small circular window overlooking the water where I'd watch seiners, potentially with Ed on board, cruise toward the fishing grounds off Tugidak Island. Sometimes I licked the glass, moving my tongue over the shape of the seiner. Anyone downstairs could tell if I had retrieved something from Maureen's desk; anyone downstairs could tell when I walked over to the small circular window.

Now, from my place by the sink, I could tell from one deep creak and a series of slighter ones that Erin had left her bed and was walking over to her bedroom window. Polly hadn't looked up from the dachshund; she was cupping its snout and saying, "Who's a Judy, Judy, Judy?" And Erin was at the bedroom window upstairs, looking out onto the Small House.

·

Polly had become useless, alternately enraged or limp. She had the acute look of pain of someone whose future was being torn in front of them, ripped from the glue of the spine.

And she was still a terrorist. She had pretended to attend to the lettuce in the Greenhouse, but instead pulled them up in handfuls. Irate, she came into the Bake Shop with her shirt-front stretched out, full of grubby shoots. She sat on the counter, eating lettuce mirthlessly.

"I'm going to fill the breast pocket of Stu's vest with deer shit," she said.

Later, I secretly took Stu's vest from where it hung in the mudroom and hung it in the gear shed.

·

That night, no one slept except for maybe Chef, who could have been doing anything in his tent cabin in the middle of the alders. I could hear someone opening the door to Erin and Polly's room, running water, and blowing her nose repeatedly. When I went out, the hall was dark; the door to Polly and Erin's room was closed again, but with light illuminating the frame.

From the window, I could see that the porthole window of the Small House was illuminated. The kitchen door opened; Erin walked out and stood at the entrance to the gravel path that led up to the cabins. She walked back, the kitchen door closed, but she didn't come up the stairs again. The sound of springs and a lever: she was in the recliner. There was another honk of nose blowing, and then my door opened.

"Can I come into your room?" said Polly, her voice so small and bright.

She sat on the bed that had been Claire's, her hands clasped over her toes. She was wearing pink pajamas. In the course of the summer, she had become ten years younger. Her chin was resting on the tops of her knees.

"Hi," I said, because it was the only thing I could say, and she said, "Hi," and her voice cracked on the "i," and she started crying again. Her nose was as pink as her pajamas.

"I want to sleep in here from now on," she said.

"That's fine," I said, and I went to her, and she curled up with her head in my lap, and all I could do was stroke her hair and say, "That's fine." Her face made the leg of my pajamas wet.

"It's not that bad, is it?" I said, and she said, "But last summer he said he loved me," and I said, "Did he? That's terrible."

·

Chef and I were sent on an errand to Kodiak. The real errand, of course, was to get out from underfoot while the screaming continued in the Small House.

Maureen called our trip "a journey into town," as if Chef and I were crossing ice floes, scrabbling for seal meat and hardtack. Our mission: stay at the Inn By The Harbor. Go to Walmart and pick up supplies. Check off the list—she gave me a list, folded and stuffed into a plastic bag for safekeeping. Talk to Adam at Deliveries. Tell him to box it up and bring it to the Susie B. in the morning.

"Maybe you can go to the movie theater," said Maureen. She was turning magnanimous. "Grab a latte. The Brown Bear Bakery has good muffins."

"For me," said Chef, "I'm looking forward to Taco Bell."

"And don't talk to the men on the tender when they go through Marmot Pass," she said. "That's especially dangerous."

I was looking forward to the men on the Susie B. I was hoping for a boat full of men who looked exactly like Ed. I couldn't wrap my head around sex on a boat, so we all stayed at Lavender Island.

Late at night, we'd go to the water line and I'd be surrounded by Eds, eight hands from Ed, sliding boots in the mossy patches by the water line, back against an alder, maybe some rope for good measure, arms flexing but with a soft tongue.

But I was a little worried, because it wasn't time to go to Kodiak yet. That was not my plan. It was too early; I wasn't ready.

It was my intention that the summer was to be for the creation of my future—yes, I'd meet with Ed; yes, our eyes would lock, I'd fumble ecstatically with the band of his sweatpants, and I'd live forever after in Kodiak. But not until November. I wasn't ready. I hadn't figured out what I'd needed to figure out about sleaze.

•

Neither of us spoke to the men on the tender as we went through Marmot Pass. Chef was enjoying the bluebird day, his pant legs rolled up to expose his calves and his head thrown back. I sat in the shade near the cabin, peering inside whenever no one was looking.

The tender was full, riding low toward town. A few pimply

deckhands had removed their Xtratufs and crawled off for a nap, exhaustion blooming beneath their eyes.

One deckhand remained, a goose-looking guy with a large Adam's apple and no chin, pink skin. He was up and about, ambling. He'd nod whenever he came in and out of the cabin—when the cabin door opened, it released a smell of sleeping bags, and Doritos, and damp, and an unwashed man smell. I was bored; I tried to catch the smell and lie back in the paralysis of lust, but it was too old and too mottled and too diffuse. The part of the smell that was Doritos overpowered the rest of it.

What bit of the cabin I could see was plain but shipshape—blond wood cupboards locked against the swells, a tiny TV playing a movie that I later identified as *Lonesome Dove*. There was a calendar marked up with "X"s and dates and times that had pictures of women in bikinis holding fish.

The goose-looking deckhand came out with mugs of coffee for me and Chef in one hand and a big container of hazelnut Coffee mate in the other. The poor deckhand had sleep in his eyes and smelled like coffee; he had been awake for a while. He had a thin voice.

"Next time, man, I'm going to be on a seiner. That's where the real money is. None of this bullshit, man. It's all the same: no sleep, but you're just cruising along, no one takes you seriously. You can't be green and on a tender. I'm from Idaho."

He wasn't even Alaskan. His hands weren't callused. I did not want to roll around with him at the top of the water line.

"Man, it's good cause you have lots of nice stuff, but guys don't take you seriously if you're not getting your hands dirty. You're not getting a workout, even. You're just awake. If I knew it was going to be like this, I would have stayed in Idaho. I can be a crane operator back home." He looked into the cabin. "This is a good movie, though."

He went inside, out of the bluebird day, to lean against the cabinet and nod off in front of the TV.

•

Maureen had booked us two rooms at the Inn By The Harbor, which sounded grand, because I was used to simplicity in naming signaling luxury, especially in accommodations, but which was, in fact, just an inn by the harbor. At the check-in desk, I realized it was mainly for fishermen: the floor was industrial linoleum with a pattern that resembled scrambled eggs. You never knew whether a green deckhand from Seattle would forget to take off his boots at the door and track fish gurry across the lobby.

The linoleum floor continued, up the stairs and into my room, which was wood-paneled and had a framed black-and-white picture of a fishing boat steaming out of harbor. The windows, had they been facing the water, would have shown the same picture, in color. But my windows were facing the mountain. On the bedside table, a map of Kodiak, a phone, and a Kodiak Island Borough phone book.

I found Ed's number. It was a local number, and I could call him for free.

And if I lost my nerve, I could just hang up. I could just hear his voice, hang up, and then call again in November. The phone was pale green, chosen to match the bedspread. I drank a glass of water. I lay on the bed and then sat up, because I'd heard that when you sat up your voice sounded more impressive. My breath was as loud as the ringing. It rang six times, then seven, then eight.

Of course: he was gone. It was peak salmon fishing season, and he was probably out on a seiner.

·

In every room for tourists, I see the echoes of Lavender Island. People, it seems, like thick pale wood. They like seeing a triangle of toilet paper folded on the roll: even I've grown to expect it. I've also grown to appreciate the loop of paper around the toilet seat cover that proves how thoroughly it's been cleaned. People like proof of the identity of the area they're visiting: at least one map on the bedside table or dresser, a piece of art with a picture of a famous landmark.

I turned my TV to an Anchorage news channel and lay there, watching a story on a tender run aground near Ketchikan, until I fell asleep.

·

The previous summer, the first night I stayed at my aunt's cabin, I was awoken by the sounds of a fox, which screams like a woman being stabbed repeatedly—all phlegm and diaphragm.

I had gone to bed that first night after setting up my room: stacking my clothes neatly, hanging my stocking cap on a hook, thumbtacking photos to the window frame, lining my windowsill with lotions and a stack of books and gel roller pens and colorful notebooks. There was something immersive and full of wonderment about setting everything just so, like making fairy houses out of moss and twigs, with a bay leaf for a doormat and acorn caps for cups.

That's maybe why the sound of the foxes was so appalling: they came into a place that was already hazy with something from childhood, where the pretty was so pretty that it made you grit your teeth and the horrible so nightmarish it made you shut and shut and shut again, like a puzzle box. I did what you do when you're frightened in the dark as a child: I stayed very, very still and—after the first scream made me open my eyes enough to register where I was, the neat parade of possessions on the windowsill—I kept my eyes closed.

When I heard the door to my room open and shut, I kept my eyes closed and prepared for whatever it was to do whatever it would do. The inevitable, I remember thinking, was that it would just stand there immobile and faceless at my bedside and I wouldn't realize until twelve hours had gone by and the sun hadn't risen that the sun would never rise again.

But then, concurrent with the screaming, was another voice, saying, "Mira. Mira, honey. Are you all right?" And then, with my eyes still closed, my marvelous aunt sat down on my bed and said, "It's only a fox. They're horrible." She stroked her hand over my hair, and I cried the very hot tears that come with relief. The next day—she really was marvelous—she made light of it. "It's a sound that makes you want to piss your pants," she said, drinking coffee in the sterile morning light, stretching her feet out in their darned socks. And I laughed—it was true, and I had not pissed my pants.

·

Chef knocked politely on my door, and looked down when I opened it with my hair all matted from sleep. He must have been as embarrassed as I was. Maureen, with great decency, had booked us rooms at opposite ends of the Inn By The Harbor, or maybe it was segregated by sex anyway, because fishermen are rough and the woman at the check-in desk had the puritanical air of the proprietress of an old-fashioned boardinghouse.

Chef didn't say anything for a moment, and then opened the zipper of his backpack. "I got a steal on this Bob Kramer knife," he said. "Some cook off a seiner was flying out and couldn't pack this in his carry-on." He unrolled a strip of felt and unsheathed a knife from a guard put together with cardboard and masking tape.

"Look!" said Chef. When I didn't respond excitedly enough, he said, "They usually go for two hundred, but this guy sold it to me for forty."

"Oh!" I said. "It's really nice."

Chef smiled and said, "It's a *beauty*."

.

Tucked inside the plastic bag next to the shopping list, were directions on how to get to Walmart. But I already knew where Walmart was. I didn't need the map. I had been there with my aunt to get supplies for her cabin. Chef and I could walk there together. It was almost exactly a year, I realized, since I had flown back from my aunt's cabin.

The sun was hidden behind a layer of moving, lichen-like cloud. The gray light reflected off more gray: the pea gravel in the lots, the corrugated siding of industrial buildings, their sloped tin roofs. Where the gray utility of the town ended, either the green mountain began its shockingly steep ascent or the sea sat there, flat and also gray.

The sheen of the cement burned my eyes even under the cloud cover, and it seemed incredibly dangerous were I to fall. And it was bewildering to encounter cars again. They were so fast, and they were somehow smaller than I had remembered them being. There was also the issue of pavement, which was hard on the soles of my feet.

Chef was in better health than he looked, or his legs were really just that long. We hurried along so quickly that I needed to watch my feet move along the sidewalk, but I looked up at every approaching footstep or the sound of tires rubbering along on wet concrete. I was scanning, out of habit, for Ed. Ed would see me with Chef; he would assume Chef was my older lover; he would punch Chef; he would take me home.

Chef and I crossed the small downtown; we passed Katmai Dry Goods. The gravel in the parking lots twinkled. We passed the intersection of Broad and Sitka; if you wanted to go to Ed's apartment, you would turn right here.

After Walmart, I could turn left here. I'd knock. I'd come in; he'd stand. "Hello, Ed." Maybe Ed would be in Walmart already? He'd pull me into the bathroom; he'd grab my hair.

"In Pahrump"—Chef's voice soured my lust—"we had the Walmart Supercenter."

The air above the Walmart was punctuated by bald eagles, just like Claire said. They congregated there in greater numbers than by the docks. Ed wasn't in the Walmart parking lot. He wasn't in the aisles. There was just me and Chef, who kept looking at the grocery list.

"This is it?" he kept asking. "This is all of it?" He flipped the paper over and over. "There isn't more?"

When we talked to Adam from Deliveries, it was clear that was all of it. There wasn't more. The dry goods that were to last us for three months fit into two large boxes.

Chef waited until we were outside. "That's not enough to last us through August, let alone through to November. You know what this means?" he asked me.

I shook my head.

"They're going under." He lit a cigarette. "They're letting us all go. Mid-season! It's mid-season!"

·

We sat at the bar at J.J.'s, and Chef made it his task to get as drunk as possible as quickly as possible. His face went gray, and his hands trembled so much that he had a hard time picking up his French fry. He drank huge tumblers of J&B whisky.

I went to the pay phone and dialed Ed's number again. The mouthpiece of the phone smelled like beer. There was no answer. Ed wasn't there. And, I thought, looking down at my sneakers crusted with spots of batter, even if he were home, he might not remember me.

Back at the bar, Chef was slumped and muttering about Lavender Island letting us go. His eyes rolled back until they were little white slits, like fingernail clippings. Chef's drunkenness impressed me with the same howl of loneliness I'd felt at the sound of empty tetherball chains hitting tetherball poles on the blacktop after school. I missed something terribly, and it took me a moment to realize that what I was missing was my Alaskan life, the one that was supposed to start in November.

A conclusion came to me through the cigarette smoke and the classic rock on the jukebox and the Christmassy light of the beer signs. What was going—what was gone—was my future in Kodiak.

I hadn't lost this future, not exactly. It's just that it was bound away. It was suspended there—my life-to-be, out of reach. And, because I'd imagined it so many times, over and over again, in so many fantasies, it was as good as being in my past.

Chef, opening his eyes enough that I could see his irises flick back and forth—the room was shuttering back and forth for him, and there must have been at least two of me—said, "You, you'll be fine. God, you're young."

It's true, I thought. There were still a million directions of possibility. There was time. There were going to be other bars with beer signs and other islands. There were going to be men. There were going to be any number of futures.

This night, I sat on my bar stool thinking, was going to be one of those swallowed up by a great clattering domino line of others. The giddy invulnerability of possible outcomes engulfed me. I felt benevolent in the face of this: there was so much sleaze to come.

I looked from face to face in the bar—Chef's eyes had rolled back again, so I didn't want to look at him—beaming with beneficence. I grinned blindly in the direction of the bartender with his snub nose, and at the group of women by the pool table.

By the jukebox were a couple of fishermen. One had a sparse

beard and an earring. One was spitting chew into a plastic water cup. They were both drunk in an expansive, opulent fashion, crowing in union, "Oh! Yeah!," as the song "Magic Man" came on. The earring one did a little jogging dance; he was too excited to sit still. Before the line "He's a magic man" came on, they both started humming in unison. The way they were beaming, you could tell they thought the song was about them.

I smiled at the smiling fishermen, allowing them the pleasure of their foolishness. I knew, of course, that the song wasn't about them. It was sung by me, in memory of Ed.

.

It was necessary to cart Chef back to the Inn By The Harbor. The bartender asked me gently, when the white crescents of Chef's eyes had finally closed and his hand lay peacefully among his French fries, whether I would take my friend home.

"He's not my friend!" I said. "He's my Chef."

"Whoever he is, sweetheart," said the bartender, "he needs to be horizontal."

The two fishermen, feeling charitable because of their belief that they were magical men, came over.

"Up you go," they said to Chef. "Up, up, up!" They slung his arms around their shoulders.

He roused himself a little as soon as we got outside. The docks were giddy. A group of exhausted-looking greenhorns were smoking a blunt by the waterfront.

"I sealed this with salmonberry jam," said one.

"That's why it's so fucking *sweet*," another said.

Chef started coughing, and one of the fishermen supporting him said, "We've got to lie him on his belly."

"We're staying at the Inn By The Harbor," I said.

"Cool. We're going to find his keys real quick." When they emptied Chef's jacket pocket, they found a bag from Taco Bell along with his room key. The fisherman with the earring put the bag into his own pocket.

"Drunk tax," he said to me, winking. "You don't get to pass out without someone stealing your shit or drawing a dick on your face. Plus, I'm hungry."

"Got to pay the tax," agreed the other fisherman.

Chef started singing something.

"Hey, a Johnny Cash fan!" said the bearded fisherman. "I've been everywhere, man."

•

Chef slept on the deck of the Susie B. all the way from Kodiak to Lavender Island. He tightened the drawstrings of his hoodie until it covered his eyes. He was trembly and pale and smelled sour, and didn't say anything about the walk back from J.J.'s, or the fishermen ("We'll take him from here," they said, walking the other way from me down the corridor of the Inn By The Harbor.) The goose-looking guy from Idaho was watching *Lonesome Dove* again. When we got in sight of the Wilderness Lodge, I had to shake Chef awake.

Maureen greeted us briskly, with a flat affect. Whatever had happened on Lavender Island while we were in town, she now looked like a black-and-white photo of herself.

"I hope town was relaxing," she said. "The guests have requested venison for dinner."

•

The Germans were interested in large animals: halibut and deer and bears. They came equipped with new fatigues and a sense of wonder at the sharp mountains going gray up top. Their directives were very clear: any halibut weighing less than a hundred pounds was undesirable. They wanted to see a bear. They had binoculars in leather cases, and they seemed intent on the art of waiting.

There were two tall, skinny men and one short, fat one. The short one bounded between the other two like a terrier, and would stop presumptuously below one or the other's nose with his hands at his hips and make the taller man lean down over him. This could have been a display of power on the part of the short one, or a weak attempt to grasp it.

They spoke impeccable, ponderous English. I never got their first names; they were written on the calendar as Müller!!!—one exclamation mark for each man.

"Is this the time for baby bears?" asked one of the tall ones.

"No, no!" said Maureen. "It's too late in the season for that. The babies are born in spring."

"Naturally," said a tall one. "But are they so big that they're identical to the big bears? The adults?"

"The mothers are ferocious in the spring, you know," said Maureen. "They don't call protective mothers 'mama bears' for nothing!"

"I see," said the tall one. "They're all adults."

"But the nice thing about Alaska," said Maureen, "is that it doesn't matter what the weather's like. We go out when it's misty, and we go out when it's a bluebird day, all the same. There's no bad weather in Alaska, only bad clothing!"

"I think our clothing will be warm enough," said a tall one, plucking at his vest.

Maureen smiled this way and that before arriving at a good idea. "Beer?" she asked.

"We prefer wine," said the short one, speaking for them all.

As it happened, the Germans' preference for wine was fortunate. All the beer in the Beer Creek had gone missing, as had all the beer in the pantry. I thought it was Polly at first, but then I saw Chef. His face regained color, then blossomed with alcohol rosacea, then went gray. He sang as he cooked dinner, but left for his tent cabin before the food was fully cooked.

·

I have never been to Alaska in the winter. In fact, I have never been to Alaska in the late fall, or early enough in the spring to be wary of mother bears. For all the changes in the Alaskan summer—the lupine into fireweed, the gaining and loss of minutes of light every day—I don't think there's as much change in the winter. There is dark, and deeper dark, and dark shot through with the aurora borealis, and there is snow giving way to patchy snow and little creeks sunk in with ice.

But all of that is conjecture. What I know is that by the time the Germans came there was fireweed on the graying hillsides, and the bioluminescence had left the water, and the salmon were beginning to peel in the rivers, strips coming off them like off a roast chicken. It was such sumptuous change.

.

My students at JSP English Academy don't know that I've never been to Alaska in the wintertime, though they certainly know more about the summer: the molting salmon, excessive light, etc. I have a picture of snowy Denali pinned to the corkboard above my desk. I've spoken about the beauty of Alaskan wintertime. They may even have the understanding that I've done something extravagantly, winterly Alaskan. Mushed?

My current students are nine-year-olds, an age group I have a great fondness and aptitude for. They're old enough to read, not too old to scoff at outings and crafts. I infuse the classroom with American culture, just as I promised Principal Jeong I would. I explain to my students the details of the Homestead Act. We've made pie crust and sourdough bread, American favorites. "Here's a scary story," I say in a low voice, turning off the overhead and lighting candles. "One day, a man named Jebediah came to Kodiak Island." We took a class trip: a hike in Juwangsan National Park. At the summit of Janggunbong Peak, I instructed the students to close their eyes and imagine that they were in the middle of a wilderness filled with bears, very, very far away from any other humans. The nearest neighbors are twelve miles away. The nearest town with a streetlight? Eighty.

## CHAPTER 10

You couldn't hunt sleaze, I'd decided. It didn't work that way. Sleaze crept after that which opposed it. If sleaze found you, it was because it was attracted to your reticence, like a cat. And there was no faking it. I'd have to become truly repulsed by sleaze, or I'd only ever attract a facsimile.

And, once I'd committed to it, I was a little shocked at how pleasurable wholesomeness was. It wasn't simply satisfying, although every small task completed—running hot water through the bacon grease in a pan—builds up to a sense of the righting of wrongs. The really nice thing about the unending negotiation of work is a sense of pleasurable remove. When you're bustling, the outside world tends to intrude only as a series of incidents, manageable chores on a list that can be checked off.

I saw that Chef had unpacked his Bob Kramer knife. It lay near the open cookbook slotted with plastic-sheeted recipes. But Chef was nowhere to be found—he'd left the kitchen with a pot of water boiling and scrambled eggs charring in the skillet. I turned off the boiling pot. Chef had forgotten to put in the potatoes. I put bread in the toaster, and whisked more eggs for scrambling.

On the windowsill was a big silver salmon in a buttered pan. There were a few flies padding around its eye, and more flies were bumping against the kitchen window. Chef had been playing *Johnny Cash Greatest Hits* on repeat since coming back from Kodiak. The VHF radio crackled over "Get Rhythm." Polly didn't come down for breakfast.

I served the eggs with chopped chives, saying, "Chives from our Alaskan garden!" The Germans clinked their silverware amicably.

Maureen sat with her arms drawn into her fleece vest, staring at her plate of eggs. I said, "We do have a very large garden! We grow all sorts of things there!" I looked over at Maureen, who stayed motionless. The Germans needed refills; I went to get the coffeepot.

Erin came into the kitchen to collect the brown-bag lunches for that day's fishing expedition. Her cheeks were pink, and the light caught the upper wisps of her hair in a sudden auburn burst. Her eyes were also pink—she had been crying, I thought, probably over most of the last few days. While I had been in town, she had been crying in the shower and in the sunroom and outside the Small House, while Maureen screamed at Stu until her voice grew hoarse.

But the pinkness rimming Erin's eyes glowed like light through an ear. She was so remote with love that the rules of beauty no longer applied to her. Polly's pinkness made her into an infant, a damp little clenched fist. Erin became a rosy princess.

When I filled the Germans' coffee cups, they seemed cheerier. I gestured the coffeepot toward Maureen, her elbows poking the baggy front of her vest like wings, but she didn't look up.

If only my aunt had behaved like this, I thought. If only she had sulked and looked into her own misery while pretending to look into a plate of eggs, I could have comforted her, or brought in a bouquet.

Maureen reacted to something, some signal that shocked her face into reaction. Her hands came out of her vest, and she turned toward the Germans.

"I hope you have a wonderful day halibut fishing," she said. "I wish I could join. But I have to do things here."

"Work on a homestead is never finished!" I said brightly from the doorway.

"Homes?" said one of the tall Germans. "Excuse me. Homes?"

"A homestead!" I said. Maureen was slowly stacking her cutlery on her plate. "This lodge was an original homestead." Maureen didn't pick up my cue. I heard the door of the mudroom slam shut; Erin was leaving before Maureen could come into the kitchen. "Like a—you know the word 'homestead'?"

"Heimstatt, oder?" said the short one. To me, he said, "This means, perhaps, 'the place where you belong'?"

•

Chef hadn't reappeared. As I washed the dishes, the Germans went back to their cabins to get cameras; as I washed the dining room windows, I could see them, along with Erin and Stu, getting into their rain gear and then skiffing out. Standing at the tiller, Stu put his hand on Erin's neck, briefly stroking the feathery hair that grew in at the nape. If I could see this, I realized, so could Maureen. She was probably watching from the porthole window of the Small House.

Upstairs, Polly was lying on the bed that had been Claire's. She was still sleeping. The air was close again, the closeness of two bodies, but it was thick with the tropical floral of Polly's bodywash, and of the lotion that promised to smell like sunripened raspberry.

•

I woke up from my nap to the sound of a clatter, followed by a yelp, followed by another clatter. Looking out the window, I saw that Chef had careened into the woodpile.

He bent stiffly to replace the chopped wood, lost his balance, and fell forward on his hands. He paused like that, suspended, in a four-legged crouch. For a second, it looked like he might bound onto the woodpile like a cat. Instead, he decided to sit down. He sat cross-legged, folded quite neatly, and reached with one arm to stack the wood. It was a haphazard job. What he had stacked wasn't coordinated with the rest of the woodpile at all, and I could tell the tarp wouldn't stretch to cover all of it.

Chef got to his hands and knees, and then up to standing, and turned to walk slowly back to his tent cabin. Polly was still curled, still asleep. When I'd finished my nap, I thought, I'd have to go and straighten up the woodpile.

·

When I finally woke up and left the room, Polly was coming up the stairs. She was still dressed in her pajama bottoms and the sweatshirt with the field-hockey elephant. She was carrying a plastic honey bear.

"Polly," I said, when she passed me, "you should get dressed." She shot me a look.

"It's pretty late," I said. She veered, not toward our room, but to the one she'd shared with Erin. I followed her, alert.

"What are you doing, Polly?"

She didn't answer.

"What are you doing with the honey?" I followed her up. She was sitting on her bed.

"I had the thought," she said, "of pouring honey in Erin's suitcase. It'll attract bugs. When she opens her suitcase, it'll be crawling."

"Maybe," I said, "although what bugs? Maybe just flies." I hadn't seen any ants all summer. "Are there even ants in Alaska?"

"There are ants," said Polly. "There are carpenter ants." She squeezed the honey bear like a hand trainer. Her eyes were the eyes of a very small and maybe hungry child.

"Polly," I said. "Carpenter ants eat wood."

"Anyway," she said, pumping the honey bear. "I also poured honey in the sunroom, and behind the couch. I hope some kind of insect invasion happens. I hope it's *crawling*. I hope it's *swarming*."

"Polly."

"I fucking hate it here," said Polly. "Stu is the Bullshit King. And Maureen is an old fucking mop. And Erin"—her voice had been getting louder and louder, and here it cracked, and she was pink again, a wavering little girl with a chin that actually dimpled in rage—"Erin's a *joke*. She was a *joke*." She threw the honey bear against the floor. It bounced, and I kneeled to grab it.

"I think you should go home," I said.

"Fuck!" said Polly. "How many times do I need to fucking say it? I need money to get to Southeast Asia!"

•

I went downstairs. Ruby or Judy was already lapping up the honey from behind the couch, feet paddling in joy. I could hear the force of the dachshund's swallowing, the hollow wet reverberation in its muzzle.

I got a bucket of sudsy water and got to work in the sunroom, moving the sponge like a spatula against the linoleum to scoop up the honey. An Arctic fly had already drowned in one of the flat pools.

The abrasive side of the sponge was soon matted with threads of cold honey. From upstairs, I heard the dull smack of Polly's fist hitting the bedroom door.

•

I was stacking up the firewood in neat columns when Chef appeared again. He must have been napping. He'd sobered up a bit; he wasn't at the point of drunk where his face turned gray. Instead, he was gregarious.

"Mira!" he said. "Hello!"

"Hi, Chef," I said.

"Carry on!" he said, and then turned again. "I hear the skiff! They're bringing back the fishies!"

"Yes indeed," I said.

He walked to the mudroom, saying, "Fishy, fishy, fishy, *fishy*!"

·

The song continued inside, where Chef was chopping potatoes with his Bob Kramer knife. It had changed; now it was "Spuddy, spuddy, spuddy, *spuddy*." From the side of the couch, the haunch of Ruby or Judy was still wriggling with joy. I was plating cheese and crackers, opening a bottle of Chardonnay. Out the window, I could see that Erin and Stu were transferring the Germans, coolers, and several large halibut from the larger fishing boat to the small aluminum skiff. Stu's hand was back playing with Erin's hair as they motored to shore.

•

Polly wasn't coming down, I realized. And there was no motion from the Small House. There was no Maureen, no hands slotted into the pockets of her vest, ponytail swinging, ready to help out. Stu was slowly hefting the halibut over to the fish-cleaning table, Erin was helping the Germans with their rain gear, washing off chum stains and errant iridescent scales with handfuls of water cupped from the bucket. Two of the Germans kept trying to help Stu with the fish, and he was waving *No, no, no* to them. They were guests, on vacation—they should be looking forward to wine.

I grabbed the bottle of Chardonnay, three wineglasses, the corkscrew. The cheese would wait.

"Chef," I said, "I'm going down."

"Down, down, downtown," he said.

•

The Germans sat on the big log by the firepit in the symmetrical order of a family portrait—tall and skinny, short and fat, tall and skinny. They drank Chardonnay and spoke in low voices, watching Stu and Erin working at the cleaning table, watching me hanging up the guest Grundéns, the real fishermen rain gear, the kind that real fishermen wear. I wondered if they liked the atmosphere: probably, I decided. It fit into an idea of America: the man cracking his knuckles and smiling down at his young bride as she filleted fish. What's more American than a desire to claim the virginal? A low clank from the skiff reminded me of the sound of Polly's fists against the wood paneling upstairs in the Big House.

One of the Germans had the idea to put the recorked bottle into what used to be the Beer Creek and now was just a cold spring creek that emptied out in eddies onto the beach.

"Are Maureen or Polly coming down?" Stu asked me. Erin's head was bowed over the table of fish, orange-gloved hands working.

"You know, I don't know!" I said. "Should I ask them?" My back was to the Germans, but my voice needed to be sparkly. Stu, whose face was turned toward the Germans, smiled.

"Let them relax," he said. "Why don't you see if our guests are interested in having some hors d'oeuvres? Maybe they're hungry?"

"Like a wolf," said one of the Germans.

There was the sound of purposeful stomping coming down the path.

"Stu," Maureen said. She even nodded at the guests. "Ruby's sick. Ruby's puking."

Stu, laughing for the Germans, a big *nothing's wrong ha ha ha,* said, "Oh, it's okay. Ruby's one of the dogs. Dachshund—that's a German name."

"Badger," said one of the Germans, and Maureen said, louder, "It's not okay, Stu. Ruby's sick. Ruby's very sick. What did she eat?"

"Badger?" said Stu to the Germans, and Maureen said, "Listen to me, Stu. This is your dog. This is *your dog.* This is the dog you supposedly love, and it's sick, and it might be dying, and you're supposed to care."

Stu spread his hands wide—*What can you do?*—for the Germans, and Erin chimed in, "I hope she didn't eat anything poisonous!" and Maureen turned to Erin and said, "You. You shut the fuck up."

"Hors d'oeuvres!" I said. "What a wonderful idea. Would you gentlemen like to come with me and have some cheese?"

"There's no reason to use that kind of language with Erin," said Stu, still in his plummy host voice, and Maureen said, exhausted beyond tears, "There is every reason in the whole wide world."

One of the tall Germans grabbed the corked bottle from the Beer Creek and said, "I think we'll need this." The other tall German said to me, "Cheese? Before dinner?"

As we walked up the hill, I could hear Maureen saying to Stu, "You have no idea how to love anything."

·

I fanned out the crackers on a plate. I brought in a new bottle of white. The cheese cubes and the salami coins I took from two plastic bags of prepped cheese cubes and salami coins marked, in Sharpie, with the date of the bagging.

I'd corralled the Germans into the dining room, even though hors d'oeuvres were normally served in the living room. They sat at the dining table I had set for dinner. I didn't want them to spend too much time looking at Chef, who had found something else to drink, something potent that smelled sweetish, maybe like almonds. When we came in, he'd been leaning heavily against the counter, flipping through a cookbook at a speed that meant he wasn't reading, just flipping. There was a tiny yellow splotch of something on his chef's jacket that had then been scrubbed with so much water that the entire double-buttoned panel was wet.

"I'm going to leave you for just a second and go check on dinner!" I said, and the Germans nodded.

In the kitchen, I turned on the CD player—calm before-dinner Bach. Chef was propping himself up against the kitchen counter, head bent forward, arms straight and locked at the elbow. I pulled over one of the bar stools with a squeak. "Chef," I said, tapping his shoulder, "take a seat."

I wasn't altogether sure he knew who I was when he looked at me. I reached to unbutton his wet chef's jacket, and he swatted at my hand petulantly. "Look," I said, whispering to keep my voice below the Bach, "this thing is all wet. Take it off." I pushed his hand away and started unbuttoning. I walked around him, slipping the jacket off arms that had, I noticed, sagging, dry elbows. I had a passing impulse to grab some Vaseline and nourish them but no, the Germans were in the dining room, and I could hear Maureen's yelling begin to arc up from the beach; there was only time to ball up Chef's wet coat, wipe at a yellow splotch that was also, I noticed, on his chin, turn up the Bach, run to throw the chef's jacket in the laundry, and get back to the guests.

They were sitting, hunched in the way of a quiet but important meeting, and perked up when I came in. I asked if they wanted more cheese. But no, what they wanted was to leave Lavender Island Wilderness Lodge early.

One smiled apologetically and said, "It is the best thing for us and for you. That is what we believe."

"Of course," I said.

"It makes sense. For everyone," said another, and I was about to say something about the forecast—more bluebird days, really very good weather, especially for this late in August—when the Bach from the kitchen stopped with a snap, the CD player whirred, and Johnny Cash started pouring out of the speakers.

"It makes sense for everyone," repeated the German, speaking above the sound of "Understand Your Man" and also Chef singing along, half a beat behind.

"I'll be right back!" I said, holding up a finger to signal one minute. I trotted to the kitchen and ducked my head around the corner.

"Chef!" I said.

He had perked up and was crushing garlic cloves with the flat end of his Bob Kramer knife, bobbing his head from side to side. From behind me, the Germans filed out of the dining room.

"We talk with Stu," said one of the tall ones.

"I can get him," I said. The others were already in the mud-room, putting on their jackets and shoes. One of them said, "Maybe it is possible to leave tonight?" and I said, "Well, maybe tomorrow will—" and the short one said, "Tonight is best," and one of the tall ones had paused in the kitchen, and Chef was saying, "I got this knife off a guy who couldn't pack it in his carry-on," and the German pulled up the bar stool with a squeak and sat down with his knees wide and said, "Maybe I can offer you a glass of water?"

I followed the short German and the other tall one out as far as the hot tub. Stu and Maureen's argument had become a low shudder of static coming from the beach. From the loudspeakers, "Understand Your Man" started again: in changing the CD, Chef had hit repeat.

"I'm sorry," I said to the Germans, as I halted by the hot tub. "I'm sorry your stay wasn't as pleasant as possible." The short one smiled at me, and then they crunched away and I watched them go. When I turned around, I saw Polly's face at the upstairs window. I waved to her.

.   .   .

What I think I saw next was a sparkle from within the kitchen, the reflection of the already-autumnal sun against the blade of the knife as it dropped. I may have seen this; something seemed to flash, the way a bright, silent burst precedes a large detonation. Or maybe there was a sound I've forgotten: a yelp, a clatter. Or maybe what happened has stained not only the time that followed, but also a small stretch preceding it. My memory is that I walked slowly to the mudroom in trepidation; the fact of the matter may be that I was oblivious and also tired.

The other tall German was on his back. The bar stool was knocked over. Chef's knife lay on the ground—there was another flash, the sun coming out from behind a cloud and striking it. Chef was kneeling over the German unsteadily. There was a spread of blood under the olive-green pants—darker green or purple. The German saying, "Scheiße, scheiße, scheiße," and then "Ist es schlimm?" Chef, in a fit of strength, tearing the purple or deep green patch of pant leg from the German's thigh, and then recoiling—blood in a spurt, up his shirt and across his face. Chef, one hand against the wound, the hand already red and very wet, grabbing two dish towels from the handle of the oven and pressing them to the German's thigh. The dish towels: already red.

"I didn't mean to!" said Chef.

I was outside, running. Stu's and Maureen's faces were folded in anger, but when they saw me they stretched into elastic masks of alarm. Their mouths were "O"s. Their eyes were "O"s. "Something happened," I said. "Chef. The German. The knife. There's a lot of blood." We ran back. Erin, sprinting. Stu, sprinting after her.

Approaching the Big House, Stu, yelling, "Erin. Stay outside. Maureen, outside." The words, cracking out, rousing the Germans from their cabins, running down the hill in the funny way of people running down hills. The short one with his arms held out to the sides for balance.

Inside, Chef was pumping on the German's leg like a chest. The German's face was gray. Stu, with full strength, pushed Chef back away from the German's leg. He pushed aside the sodden dish towels, releasing another spritz of blood. The German, in a voice that was a little quieter than it had been before, asked the other Germans, "Ist es schlimm? Ist es schlimm?," and they crowded around his head. Stu turned to Chef, whose arms and legs splayed when he was pushed over. "Get out of my sight," he said, and Chef's face crumpled up and he started bawling. I could see all the teeth in his mouth.

Chef got up on his hands and knees, slid on the blood on the floor, got up on his hands and knees again, wavered, straight-limbed like a colt, and ran out. I saw his torso sprint past the kitchen window. Then I was already in the bathroom, getting the first aid kit. A first aid kit is a reassuring sight: all bright colors and easily marked packages. The tourniquet was orange, with a darker orange windlass rod. I went back to the bathroom, brought back a stack of towels. I threw them down around the German's leg, still folded, and watched them redden around the edges and then, in a sudden bloom, in the middle.

I was on the VHF radio. "Lavender Island Wilderness Lodge to Coast Guard," I said, and then, meek, "Please, help."

"I understand the name is Lavender Island Wilderness Lodge. Lavender Island Wilderness Lodge, this is the United States Coast Guard, Kodiak, Alaska. Over," said the metallic woman's voice.

"Help," I said. "Please. There's a man hurt."

"Coast Guard to caller. Are you in need of assistance?"

"Please!" I said, and then realized that "Understand Your Man" had started playing again. I turned the power off. "We need assistance. A man is very hurt," I said. "Can you hear me?"

Stu was twisting the windlass rod of the tourniquet. He had blood in and around one ear, I noticed—had he scratched at it? The unharmed Germans were touching their friend's face. He was asking again, "Ist es schlimm?" and his friend was telling him "Nein, nein, nein," and explaining, I think, Stu's tightening of the tourniquet and my calling the Coast Guard on the VHF.

I pushed the button on the fist mic. With the music off, I could hear the German's breathing. It sounded like a rooting baby's. "Lavender Island Wilderness Lodge to Coast Guard. A man is very hurt. His leg is cut. A knife."

Someone had kicked the knife across the floor. It was near the woodstove. I stared at it; it still looked very clean. Stu was still working at the tourniquet, but his hands kept slipping. The blood had snuck under the dam of the folded towels and was spreading with that certain viscosity between milk and syrup.

"Mein Gott," said the German, and that was the last time I saw his face. He started speaking so softly one of his friends had to put their ear next to his mouth, and then Stu said the tourniquet wasn't working, and then he took the fist mic from me, and then told me to run down to the beach, where, I realized, there was more screaming.

Chef, still sobbing, still very drunk, had tried to swim out into the water. But, because he was still drunk, and probably also because he was sobbing, it was easy for Erin and Maureen to drag him from the water and pin him down.

·

"Where's Polly?" said Maureen finally. We were sitting on the beach, waiting for the Coast Guard helicopter to arrive, just as the voice on the VHF had instructed us to.

Chef was sitting outside the gear shed. He was rocking back and forth with his eyes closed. I had gone into the Guest Cabins for blankets and had wrapped one around Chef's shoulders. He didn't seem to notice.

The Germans, a duo now, were seated back on the same log where they had drunk Chardonnay earlier. The shorter one had his head on the shoulder of the taller one. They were sharing a blanket around their shoulders and sharing one across their laps.

Stu and Erin were sitting down the beach, each wrapped in a separate blanket. Maureen was doubled over in prayer. She only stopped to look up and say, "Where's Polly?"

Polly was still upstairs in the Big House.

．

When I walked in through the mudroom, I looked purposely at the floor. I would have rather not had to look at the blood at all, but it was better to look at the swirls against the homey, warm grain of the Big House floor than to slip, lose my footing, and end up looking at the body of the German all covered in soaked towels.

Upstairs, Polly was lying on her bed, hands curled up near her face. I crouched down until my face was level with hers. "Polly," I said. "You have to get out of this house." I said it in the same hushed singsong as you would use to tell someone it was time to get up, the same voice my aunt had used when she'd told me it was only a fox. I stroked back Polly's hair.

"What happened down there?" she asked.

"We'll talk about it on the beach," I said. "Put on a sweatshirt. Do you have a hat?"

"It's in the mudroom," she said, and I thought she was going to start crying. Everyone was crying or rocking or soothing each other or talking to God, and I just needed very, very much for Polly to not cry—I couldn't take her sadness, because that would mean there was only sadness. It would crash and keep on crashing. *Ed*, I thought, *my proximity to danger is very close now*, but Polly was walking to the door, and I needed her not to see the body of the German and not to be sad or to scream or to cry.

"Polly!" I said. I took her shoulders. "Listen to me. Close your eyes. I'm going to lead you. But keep your eyes closed."

Down the stairs, she felt for each step with a white-socked foot, and I counted the stairs for her as "One, one, one, one, one, one, one." When we got to the bottom, I turned her toward the door, my hands over her eyes. I kept counting, this time for steps: "One, one, one, one."

When she stepped into the blood for the first time, her whole body shuddered, but I kept my hands so firmly over her eyes that she'd see stars later. It must have been obvious to her that there was blood—the wet floor and the sweet, brassy stink—but she didn't ask to see. She kept her eyes closed when I removed her jacket and hat and boots from the mudroom. She kept her eyes closed as I peeled the wet socks from her feet, curled them into tight red coils and threw them into the bushes, put on fresh wool socks, and helped her balance as she slid on her boots. Once we passed the kitchen windows, I told her she could open her eyes, and she ran ahead of me down to the beach.

.

I met Maureen at the Inn By The Harbor. We sat in the corner of the lobby in armchairs printed in a beige geometric pattern.

"After factoring in room and board, this is what we could spare for you," said Maureen as she gave me my paycheck. What she gave me was twelve hundred dollars. It was not enough for anything. "You understand, of course, that there were extenuating circumstances."

I did understand.

"Chef's probably going to go away for a while," said Maureen. She was touching the cord of her corduroys: soft sweater, soft sweater, soft sweater. "Imagine! Dear Lord. The knife nicked the femoral artery. But this isn't Chef's first offense. He was drunk in Idaho and ran down some old lady in his pickup."

I probably should have hugged her. Instead, I sat there and

held the check and didn't even look up until the recorded chime of the lobby door let me know she was out on the street.

·

I had thought, when I first met Maureen, that aging must be tragic because there's no longer any time to think of your futures, those luminous balloons. I thought that you could only hold those aloft if there was a possibility of them coming true one day; no one wishes on a white horse or a cat in a window for something that has already passed.

But that's idiocy. You can always return to the dreams in those balloons. It might take more time, more stillness, a duller domestic task—cleaning windows—or a longer time spent in bed before ducking under into sleep, but they're there.

Maureen must have her future with Stu still. She must have everything she saw before her when they packed up in Wisconsin. She would have walked around that bare apartment or house—I'm picturing a little house, with scuffed wood floors—to check the closets before they left. It was the seventies, so I'm imagining everything with the burnished glow of an old film.

Twenty-four-year-old Stu, leaning against the back of their van, outside. Maureen would have been an accomplished homemaker even then, a wary mistress of the house. She would have gone back to put the keys in the freezer of the unplugged refrigerator for the landlord and paused with cheerful wistfulness at their bare bedroom: it looked so much smaller without the furniture. She would have looked out the bathroom window one last time onto the deck. Then, north to Alaska.

Alaska was a place on the top of the map, outlandishly over-sized, like Greenland, but still as big as most of the continental United States. She'd have laughed, maybe in the suburbs of Calgary, at all the little homes with all the little lawns and all the little amenities and all the little cupboards and little sorrows because no one there could bear to strike out.

·

I called my parents. "I have to come back," I said. I told them I would use what was left of the twelve hundred dollars to take my GED and enroll in community college. I would get a job. I might be qualified to work as a baker.

.

My flight wouldn't leave until the next afternoon, so I stayed another night at the Inn By The Harbor. There was a drunk man in the next room who sang for a while and then vomited. It was late enough in the season that I didn't need the blackout curtains at all. The weather report on TV declared fine weather for the duration of the week.

I sat by the harbor and looked at every pair of soft pants that walked by to see if it might be Ed. There was no Ed; there was a woman that might have been my aunt getting into a car in the parking lot with a large bag of groceries. I yelled out "Hey!" but the woman didn't hear—there were a lot of people yelling "Hey!" all over the harbor. Then I remembered my aunt was dead, and remembered everything else all over again.

The Kodiak Airport had no snack bar and very little security, so I sat outside and watched the forklifts move back and forth. They were loaded down with coolers full of frozen fish from people's vacations. I thought idly: now would have been the time for Ed to show up, I'm at the airport, this is where dramatic things happen, but Ed was probably out fishing. I went down to the creek that ran alongside the parking lot and watched the tattered backs of thrashing salmon.

·

There are a couple of situations that are ideal for touring your memories: the quiet three minutes after takeoff on a commercial flight, and when you're trying to fall asleep. The first makes you keenly aware of the possibility of a quick death, and the other makes you aware of the likelihood of one that comes slowly.

As I flew out from Kodiak Airport, Ed landed at my aunt's cabin in that toy-looking yellow seaplane. He's continued to land for me in the same way most days since then. The plane, a bright stamp on a bright blue sky, dashes first right across the mountains, then swoops back left, then another right.

Of course, I can start from any number of instances: Ed hopping off the pontoon is good; Ed walking with that saunter up the shale-chip beach. But it's best to start with that first pass of his plane, from left to right across the mountains, because that's the beginning.

ACKNOWLEDGMENTS

These acknowledgments, apart from the last two, are listed chronologically. I'm detailing just the people and institutions who have directly impacted this novel; if I were to try to acknowledge everyone who has shaped me as a writer the list would be unending.

My deepest thanks:

To the Berlin Senatsverwaltung für Kultur und Europa/

Berlin Senate for Culture and Europe. Without the generous support offered through the Arbeitsstipendium für nichtdeutsche Literatur/ Working Stipend for Non-German Literature 2018, this project may never have reached completion.

To Lettrétage and Tom Bresemann, the Literarisches Colloquium Berlin, and the English Theater Berlin for hosting readings of this novel in its draft form. To Frank Sievers and Eva Bonné for their thoughtful, creative moderation. And to Martina Kohl for her tireless work supporting US-American literature in Berlin.

To the friends who read an early version of this novel and whose thoughtful comments and astute suggestions helped bring it to its eventual shape: Amy Benfer, Tom Drury, Jane Flett, Matt Gammie, Amanda Goldblatt, Jennifer Kronovet, Madeline LaRue, Carmen Maria Machado, Kannan Mahadevan.

To PJ Mark, for his advocacy and patience.

To Lee Boudreaux and Anne Meadows, for their incisive, exacting, brilliant edits.

To Foundation OBRAS (especially Carolien van der Laan, Ludger van der Eerden, and Flor) for running such a joyful residency. To Nuoren Voiman Liitto and Villa Sarkia (especially

Raija Hänninen and Laura Serkosalo) for the time and silence in which to write.

To my family: my parents, Alison and Bill Rukeyser, for their dedication and unfailing support; my brothers, Casey, Gabe, and Jacob Rukeyser for their brilliance and humor.

To Florian Leitner, who made this possible.

ABOUT THE AUTHOR

Rebecca Rukeyser is the recipient of the inaugural Berlin Senate grant for non-German literature. Her fiction has appeared in such publications as *Zyzzyva*, *The Massachusetts Review*, and *The Best American Nonrequired Reading*. She received her MFA from the Iowa Writers' Workshop and teaches fiction writing in Berlin.